THE UNICORN'S QUEST

Jonathan Soule

PublishAmerica
Baltimore

First printing

At the specific preference of the author, PublishAmerica allowed
this work to remain exactly as the author intended, verbatim, without
editorial input.

ISBN: 1-4241-2491-3
PUBLISHED BY PUBLISHAMERICA, LLLP
www.publishamerica.com
Baltimore

Printed in the United States of America

This book is dedicated to my beautiful, wonderful mother, Alice Gertrude Brower who even though she had to raise ten children virtually by herself, somehow always found time to read to us. Thank you, Mom, for the greatest of all gifts, the love of reading.

The author would like to extend a special thanks to Mrs. Ronna Hoffman and all her different Herriman Elementary third grade classes. Their endless energy, enthusiasm and encouragement are the reason this book exists today.

Chapter One

Juxtaposition

Today was getting stranger and stranger, Alyssa decided as she gazed out her living room window. From her place on the couch, she watched as a large, forest green butterfly with red circles on its wings fluttered across her front yard and perched itself atop a rose.

Alyssa had never seen a butterfly anything like this before. It's shape was that of a swallowtail's, with oval wings that had tips at the end, but it was at least twice as big as the biggest butterfly she'd ever seen. It was easily as large as a small dove. The butterfly's wings slowly flapped as it sucked nectar, and Alyssa suddenly realized that the red circles, one on each wing, with their slanted black centers, looked amazingly like eyes. Human eyes. The butterfly's wings slowly stopped, spread wide, and Alyssa gasped, a sudden chill running through her. They looked like eyes all right, blood red human eyes. Angry eyes. For just an instant, she had the strangest feeling that they were looking directly at her—and that they were after her, that they wanted to hurt her. She unconsciously shrank back from the window as the butterfly lifted from the rose.

"Mom!" she yelled over her shoulder. "You've got to come see this!"

There was a moment of silence. "Are the lights flashing again, sweetheart?" her mother asked from the kitchen. She sounded preoccupied.

"No. It's not that this time, mom. It's a butterfly like I've never seen before. And it's huge. You've got to hurry. It's flying away right now!"

However, by the time Alyssa's mom reached the window carrying her half-naked baby sister, Tahnee, the butterfly was gone.

"It flew off," Alyssa stated flatly. "You took too long."

"Oh well, I'm sure it will be back," her mom replied. "And I've probably seen it before. There are a lot of butterflies around here."

"Not like this one there's not. It was huge, and it had spots on its wings that looked like eyes."

Alyssa's mom nodded knowingly. "A buckeye butterfly. I've seen those before."

"No, mom, this wasn't a buckeye. I've seen buckeyes too. Lots of times. Buckeyes are brown, with brown spots. This was dark green with red spots. I mean, *really* red spots."

And it was kinda scary! Alyssa thought to herself but didn't add. How do you explain to someone that a butterfly had frightened you? In fact, how could a butterfly frighten you? That was just plain crazy.

Alyssa shook her head in resignation and glanced back out the window at the thin clouds where the lights had been flashing a few minutes ago. Her mom turned to go.

"If you see it again," she said as she left. "Call me, and I'll try and come back faster. In the meantime, honey, would you go find Brett? He said he was going over to the church to see if anyone was going to play ball today. Tell him that I need his room cleaned before he can play. It's a sty in there."

Alyssa sighed and shook her head. She hated having to go and look for her brother. Just then a light red, almost pink, hue swept through the clouds on the far horizon. It was quickly followed by a green one. Then baby blue. It was like a reflection of distant, unseen fireworks going off in the daytime.

"Mom, the lights are back," Alyssa called.

"That's nice, honey. Now please go find your brother."

Alyssa stood and started for the front door. She paused before she turned the handle. The lights hadn't bothered her before—she had in fact thought that they were pretty cool—nor had it scared her that her bath water this morning had come out of the tap a navy bluish color, which had slowly faded to clear. She of course hadn't bathed in it. That would be stupid. It was probably contaminated water. Who knew? But now all of it combined—especially the butterfly's eyes— was making her nervous.

"Mom, what do you really think is causing those lights?"

Alyssa heard the kitchen sink's water being turned on. "I told you, honey, it's probably something like the Northern Lights. If you really want to know, you can call the Hansen Planetarium when you get back."

Aurora borealis is what that's *called, mom. And you don't see them in the day, and not as far south as Salt Lake.* But Alyssa kept this information to herself. Her mother probably wouldn't agree, and what's more, wouldn't care. When she was busy with the baby, she and her brother could be whisked off by aliens, flown around the universe and then brought back home, and her mother would just simply discount it as a new high-tech form of travel, devised by the government. And why weren't their rooms clean? Flying around the universe was no excuse for a dirty room! She sighed in resignation as she turned the front door's handle and stepped out. Might as well just go and find her brother and get it over with.

It's a Juxtaposition, a small voice said inside Alyssa's head, and she jumped, slightly startled. She had no idea where *that* had come from! She didn't even know what that word meant! And, as freaky as it was, that hadn't *sounded* like her inside voice. Not even a little bit. It had sounded like someone else—only talking inside her head!

Closing the door, she stepped out onto the front porch, feeling really freaked out now. This was getting just a little *too* strange. Where was all this stuff coming from? And why all of a sudden, and all in one day? She shook her head. She had no idea. But she was sure of one thing; she was going to get Brett and get right back home. A hot, afternoon breeze met her as she strode purposefully to the sidewalk.

Alyssa was tall for her age, taller in fact than anyone else in her eighth grade class. Her hair was chestnut brown, perfectly straight and hung to her shoulders, and her eyes were the same color of brown, only a lighter shade. She had her mother's chin, her father liked to tell her, with a small cleft down the center, as well as her build, which was thin and somewhat fragile looking. Alyssa wasn't the most popular girl in her junior high, being shy and quiet most of the time, but by the same token she also didn't have any enemies, for pretty much the same reason. She and her best friend, Katie, were mostly content to keep to themselves—having their own *club* instead of joining one. Katie, however, did go to 4-H for horses on Saturdays, which was where she was today. Alyssa's parents said that they couldn't afford a horse, nor did they have a place to keep one or the desire to take care of it. Also, Alyssa's dad firmly believed that a person should only have a few hobbies, or *activities*, as he called them, and in their family the main *activity* was camping, hiking and rock climbing. It was his passion. Alyssa had gone hiking with him for as far back as she could remember, and he'd started her on climbing walls—*The Mall Walls,* he called them—in the second grade. He'd started Brett only a few months later. He liked to brag that she and her brother were his "Climbing Buddies".

But as much as Alyssa loved to hike and rock climb, some days she still wanted a horse, too. Katie was really lucky.

Rounding the corner, Alyssa spied Brett near the church's ball field just in front of the bleachers. He was alone and bent over something on the ground, staring at it intently.

Brett was the exact opposite of Alyssa—outgoing, aggressive, full of energy—and the spit and image of his father. He was also tall for his age, but with a heavier, more solid build. His hair was dirty blonde, almost brown, and cut very short. If he ever let it grow long, it went curly, which he absolutely hated. Brett was one of the most popular boys in the seventh grade. He played baseball, basketball, and was in a peewee football league. He was everyone's friend. Most of time he drove Alyssa nuts. He was always into her stuff and making fun of her and her friends. About the only good thing she had ever heard about him was that he'd once put his sixth-grade school bully in his place for picking on some fourth-graders. One thing their dad had drilled into both of them was that you never backed down to a bully, no matter what. Bullies were cowards. They didn't really want to fight, just beat people up. Let them know that they're in for a fight, and they'll run away as fast as they can.

As she reached the edge of the ball field, Alyssa called, "Brett, mom wants you home to clean your room. She says it's a sty. Like always."

Brett looked up and waved frantically at her. He was quite obviously very excited.

"Alyssa," he yelled back. "Come and see what I've found. It's incredible. I'm gonna be rich!"

Alyssa took a deep breath and steeled herself. Brett was always finding one-of-a-kind things, and he was always gonna be rich. Like when the first State's Quarter had come out a couple of years ago. Every single other person in America had heard about them before they came out, except Brett. Then he'd found the Delaware horse in his change and came home walking on air. He was sure it was a "one-of-a-kind" mistake from the U.S. Mint worth millions. He was gonna list it on EBay tonight! It had been with great pleasure that Alyssa had shown him the five that she'd bought from the bank that afternoon. But his dejection had been short-lived—it always was. Brett now collected the quarters in mint condition, and *that* was going to be worth a fortune someday. He really was going to sell it on EBay.

As she approached, Alyssa now saw what Brett was looking at, and it sent another shiver of fright—her second for the day—through her. Like the butterfly earlier, this was truly a one-of-a-kind. It was a flower, of sorts, like a very large daffodil—only instead of yellow petals in the center of it's green leaves, it had a miniature, true-to-life golden tiger's head, complete with yellow stripes, black eyes and very sharp-looking teeth. At the moment, the small tiger's head was growling lightly, and showing its teeth to Brett.

Feeling very lightheaded—almost as though she were going to faint—Alyssa stopped a couple of feet behind Brett and stared down in an awe that bordered on complete disbelief. Here was one more really strange thing to add to today's tally—only this one was the craziest of all!

"Watch this, Alyssa," Brett said excitedly, not noticing the scared look on her face. He plucked a long blade of grass from under the bleachers and moved it slowly toward the tigerhead. The flower crouched down on it's stem as the grass approached. When the end of the grass came within reach, the little tiger pounced on it, growling viciously, and tore it to shreds. Ripped pieces of grass flew in all directions.

"Don't mess with it, Brett," Alyssa said quietly. She wanted to get away from this. She wanted to get back home. And now. Today was getting just too whacked-out. "You should leave it alone. You don't know what it is, or where it came from. And anyways, it looks mad, and doing that is mean."

Brett snorted contemptuously. "It's not any meaner than playing string with a kitten. It likes this game. It's having fun."

"It doesn't look like it's having fun to me," she stated softly. "Now come on, you've teased it enough. Mom says you have to clean your room."

Brett stood up and stared over at Alyssa in open amazement.

"I am *not* leaving a rare Tigerflower here, just so I can go and clean my room!" he stated loudly. "Okay? Someone else will find it and take it. And I found it first, so it's mine!"

"It is not yours, Brett. It's on church property. It's the church's, if it's anybody's. And anyways, where did you here about 'Rare Tigerflowers?' I've never heard of them before. Ever. And I read ten times more nature books than you. It's probably some endangered species, or something, from Africa. You shouldn't mess with it. It might even be poisonous. We should just leave it alone, and go get dad."

"Yeah, right, like *that's* gonna happen," Brett replied as he reached into his back pocket. He brought out his Boy Scout knife and thumbed it open. "It's endangered all right—in danger of someone else taking it before I do! I'm going to dig it up and plant it again back at home. It can be 'endangered' there just as well as here."

In horror Alyssa watched as Brett knelt down and cautiously

reached forward with his knife to dig around the plant. But the tigerflower—angry, frustrated and much faster than Brett had planned—pounced quickly on his hand. It sank its small, pinlike teeth into the top of his index finger, then growled and shook it's head. Brett dropped his knife, yelled and tried to pull his hand away. But the flower was much stronger than he'd ever imagined. It hung stubbornly on to his finger as blood flowed down his hand and dripped onto the ground. Brett yelled again and pulled harder. The flower growled and bit down. Alyssa suddenly felt faint again with fear. The blood on the ground was puddling now, starting to seep into the earth.

She had to do something.

She reached down and grabbed onto Brett's hand, to help pull.

And that's when it happened.

The lights that had been flashing all morning on the distant clouds suddenly swept past her vision. Blue. Red. Green. The air sparkled and spun, like glitter in a funnel cloud. The world tilted. Brett's blood on the ground suddenly shone like a jewel. A blazing, blood-red ruby. It became her only focus. Her vision grayed. Brett's screaming became a distant sound.

It's a Juxtaposition she heard that strange voice say in her head again right before she fainted for real.

She didn't know how long she was out, but when Alyssa came to, she found herself lying in a clump of tall grass with Brett standing over her, sucking his finger and looking around. She sat up. The ball field, the church, the street—in fact *everything* was gone. In its place was a wide, rolling meadow of grass, dotted here and there with large, multicolored butterflies and tigerflowers.

"Where are we?" Alyssa gasped.

"I don't know," replied Brett quietly, almost in awe. "But I think we're gonna be in trouble when we get home!"

CHAPTER TWO

The Unicorn

For a few minutes Alyssa looked down at the tall grass while the world stopped spinning around her. She concentrated her attention on her hands, staring at her topaz and silver ring. She tried to calm her mind. This wasn't happening. It couldn't be.

Slowly she stood up, still staring down, smoothed her shirt and then glanced sideways at Brett. He was still gazing around in awe, index finger firmly planted in his mouth. She finally lifted her eyes and looked around again. The huge meadow was still there. It's tall grasses waved gently in a summer breeze that smelled faintly of salt. Most of the grass was bright green, but some of it had an almost purplish hue that changed in intensity as it blew in the wind. Dotted here and there were patches of large, colored flowers being visited by a variety of butterflies, some of which looked exactly like the green one she'd seen in her front yard. The tigerflower that had bit Brett was still watching them carefully, bright red blood glistening on it's petals, but a different one several yards further away paid no attention to them. It was busy chewing on what looked like the remains of a navy blue butterfly.

Great! Alyssa thought. *Venus flytraps to the extreme! What kind of place is this?*

In the distance, she could see a thin blue line stretching from one end of the horizon to the other. Her first impulse was to think that it was a large lake, but judging from the salty smell in the air, it was more likely an ocean. She turned and looked the other way. There, some four hundred yards away, stood a thin, park-like forest of evergreens, which went in both directions for as far as she could see. It rose into rolling, pine-covered hills on the far horizon. No people, no houses, no buildings—not even animals of any sort—were anywhere in sight. They were all alone.

"What happened, Brett?" Alyssa asked, turning to look at him. "Where are we?"

Brett took his finger out of his mouth and examined it. Small drops of blood still welled out of five pinprick-like holes.

"How would I know?" he replied defensively. "This isn't my fault you know. I didn't do it."

"I never said you did," Alyssa answered. It came out a little more tartly than she had wanted, but she *was* stressed. "For all I know, this is a dream."

Brett shook his head. "Everything's always my fault. And if this is a dream, it's a painful one. Those flowers are mean." He glared down at the tigerflower. It glared right back. "I need a band-aid. You got one?"

"No. Why would I have a band-aid?"

"I was just hoping." Glancing around, Brett spied his scout knife sticking point down in the ground next to the tigerflower. "That's some luck," he said. He kicked it out from under the flower and picked it up. He then proceeded to cut a strip of cloth from the bottom of his t-shirt and tied it around his finger, stopping the flow of blood.

"You've seen Rambo too many times," Alyssa stated in disgust.

Brett grinned. "You've gotta do what you gotta do, Lyssa."

Alyssa gritted her teeth. Lyssa was her dad's nickname for her and she hated it when Brett called her by it. Of course, Brett knew this, which was why he did it. But she refused to give him the satisfaction of complaining.

"Well, that's just it," she said. "We need to decide what to do. We can't just sit here."

"I guess you didn't bring mom's cell phone with you, did you?" Brett inquired almost casually. "I mean, just by some lucky chance."

"No. I didn't. And what makes you think it would work here

anyway?" Alyssa paused. "Wherever 'here' is."

"Oh, they work almost everywhere now. Dad and I called home from the elk hunt in the Uintas last year. We were on a mountain twelve thousand feet up and five miles from the closest road. It came in crystal clear."

Yeah but that was Earth, Alyssa thought, but she immediately chided herself. Of course they were still on earth. How could they possibly be anywhere else? Something strange had happened, something she didn't fully understand, but she wasn't going to panic. Not yet anyway. One thing that rock climbing taught you was to never panic, and always, *always,* keep moving. If you froze up and just clung blindly to a cliff wall, eventually you'd fall from exhaustion. Rock climbing taught you to take action! Move or fall. The important thing right now was to find out exactly where they were—and how to get home before it got too late!

Turning and gazing all around again, Alyssa made a decision.

"I think we should walk over to that forest and see if there's a trail. It might lead to a...a...town, or something." She had almost said *village* but stopped herself short. Village sounded almost spooky. There was no way she going to go look for *villagers.*

"Whatever," Brett replied with a shrug of his shoulders. He folded up his scout knife and put it into his pocket. "I don't think it matters, myself. If you don't know where you're at, or where you're supposed to go, one direction will be just as good as the other. And it's pretty obvious we're not going to meet someone here, so let's go."

Alyssa had no reply to that—because of course Brett was right—and so turned and started walking. The grass was almost waist high in spots, and there seemed to be no trails, but it was soft against Alyssa's legs. The afternoon sun gave off a lazy warmness—not really hot—and the only sound they heard as they walked was the occasional droning of unseen bees.

Alyssa found it was best to steer clear of the occasional patches of wildflowers. The tigerflowers were hidden down among them, awaiting their flying prey, and she had no desire to get bit like Brett.

People didn't seem to scare them at all.

As they neared the forest edge, the grass grew rapidly shorter. Upon inspection, Alyssa found that it had been clipped evenly like Katie's horse did when it grazed. A large herd of animals that ate grass lived here—or were brought here on a regular basis. The forest itself was less like a wild forest and more like a groomed park. The evergreens were evenly spaced about fifteen feet apart with two-inch high grass growing right up to their trunks. Very few fallen trees or limbs were anywhere to be seen. On one of the closer trees, a large brown squirrel with big, almost intelligent-looking eyes, sat watching them. It didn't scamper or scold, or even hardly move. It just sat and watched, as though it were debating on what it needed to do.

As she returned the squirrel's gaze, Alyssa felt Brett nudge her in the ribs and whisper, "Look over there! Do you see that?"

Alyssa turned and her breath caught in her throat. Standing about thirty feet away at the edge of the forest was the most beautiful creature she had ever seen. It was unicorn the size of a large horse. It's fur was a light, sky blue and it had four white socks that went all the way up to it's knees. The unicorn's single horn as well as its hooves, which looked like they were made of pure silver, glinted brilliantly in the early morning sunshine. It was staring intently at them, in much the same fashion as the squirrel.

"It's a unicorn!" Alyssa breathed quietly. Brett just snorted as if to say *No kidding!* The blue unicorn began to walk slowly toward them, its movements were graceful and light, and yet they gave off a sense of an incredible, hidden strength.

"What do we do?" Brett muttered.

"You should say hello," the unicorn replied. Its voice was light and musical. "That's the polite thing to do. And since my intentions here are only to help you, you should be polite. I know I would be."

Alyssa gave an involuntary squeal of fright. "It talks." Her voice was high and tight. "What do we do now?"

"I am not an it," the unicorn replied evenly as it stopped ten feet away from them. Its tone gave no hint as to whether it was honestly offended or not. "My name is Blue, and I am one of the Queen's Royal Unicorns. And a Blue one at that. I was sent here to watch the Juxtaposition. Even with war raging, Juxtaposition must be watched. Occasionally, on rare occasions, dangerous things come through, and they must be dealt with immediately. At the very least, we need to know whether something has come through or not."

Alyssa couldn't help herself. She *just* had to know.

"What *is* a Juxtaposition?" she asked shyly.

The unicorn seemed almost to smile.

"A Juxtaposition is when Tanzal, our world, the world you are in now, becomes perfectly parallel with any one of hundreds of other worlds. Sometimes they will touch in one small spot, which is called a Congruence, and things from Tanzal will sometimes *migrate* into the other world for a time. Tanzal's skies will flash with colors when a Congruence is happening. When the two worlds separate, Tanzal pulls all her parts back to herself—and sometimes other things are *pulled* back as well. I watched you appear in the meadow in a shower of magic at the end of this Juxtaposition. Something pulled you through and your world did not have the strength to keep you. It must have been very weak in magic to lose something as large as you. Tanzal is the strongest in magic of all the worlds. It never leaves anything behind in a Juxtaposition. Not even so much as a grain of sand."

Alyssa felt herself suddenly on the verge of tears. This couldn't be happening. They really weren't on earth anymore.

"How do we get back home?" Brett asked.

The unicorn stared at them for a long moment, his face almost sad. "I do not know the answer to that question. These things are beyond my knowledge or power. I know that sending things back to their own world always takes deep magic. And it doesn't always work. I do know, however, that if you stay for very long in Tanzal, her magic will begin to work on you and she will begin to consider you hers.

"And then, like her every grain of sand, she will never let you go."

Tears began to form in Alyssa's eyes. She tried to hold them back as hard as she could. This wasn't the time to start bawling.

"Who does this deep magic?" she asked timidly. "How do we find them and ask them to help us?"

Now, Blue looked down and pawed the ground.

"That is the worst part of what I must tell you," he said, still not looking up as if he were ashamed to look in their eyes. "Black times are upon Tanzal. The worst seen in a hundred generations. War, both magical and actual physical fighting, has broken out on our Northern border. A part of The Great Northern Shield has been breached. And Evil things invade. Not all magic in Tanzal is good. Normally, many creatures and at least one Wizard would watch a Juxtaposition. This time, only I am here. It would take all the resources of The Queen and the entire Wizarding Council to have a chance of sending you back. But they are engaged in battle."

The unicorn looked back up at them. His eyes glistened lightly, making them a darker shade of blue.

"I am sorry, human children, but in peacetime, we would have done all we could for you. Now, however, I dare not even contact them. A stray magical contact at the wrong moment could cause great harm. I am afraid that you might be stuck here."

Unable to stop herself, Alyssa started to lightly cry. A couple of tears rolled down her face.

"So, there's nothing we can do? Can't we try something? I don't want to stay here forever. Who would we live with?"

"There are other humans living in Tanzal. They live near the Southern Sea. Your world lost others before you, very long ago. The Queen herself has human blood in her veins, as do many of the Wizards on the council. You will be taken care of. Provided Tanzal survives this war." The unicorn paused for a moment, lost in thought. He gazed at them contemplatively.

"There is, however," he finally continued, "something we might try. The Norfs live barely a day's ride away from here, in the Rockroller Mountains. They refuse to go to war, using their powerful magic from a distance to help protect Tanzal. They do as little as can get away with, and I'm not even sure that they will help us. They actually don't much like people—or unicorns for that matter."

"What are Norfs?" Brett asked.

"They are three brothers who are closely related to the Gnomes. No one knows how old they are, but they are ancient. They are very powerful in magic, and weren't always on the side of good. Long ago, the Wizarding Council defeated them in magical battle, and bound them from evil. They usually help only when compelled, but perhaps we can make an appeal."

"Anything is better than nothing," Alyssa blurted.

"True," the unicorn replied, nodding. "However, I'm not even sure if they are strong enough to send you back. I wouldn't get your hopes up too high. It would help..." he paused and stared thoughtfully at them both.

"It would help if you had some magic of your own. I think I should test you."

"You mean I could have magic?" Brett exclaimed.

The unicorn laughed lightly. It was a high and musical and had a magical quality, like distant wind chimes on a crisp winter's night. "Every living creature has magic in it—even ants. They just don't have very much. The question is how much do *you* have. In Magic, especially Spellcasting, all the participant's magic can be combined, making the spell that much stronger. Any natural magic you might have could be a great help in sending you back. I shall test you."

The Unicorn stared at Brett. Sky-blue sparkles of light, like floating glitter, suddenly appeared in the air all around them. After only a moment, they disappeared. Blue sighed.

"It's what I was afraid of. Coming from a world weak in magic, you have very little yourself. I doubt it will be of much use." He turned and stared at Alyssa. "You are probably the same, but I shall test you nevertheless."

The Unicorn concentrated on Alyssa, and once again the sky-blue sparkles appeared in the air around them. But then something else happened. Dark green sparkles, the color of pine needles, filled the air as well. They spun around the blue ones, moving faster, getting larger, swirling uncontrollably. Suddenly, the Unicorn snorted and threw his head. The contact was broken. He took an involuntary step backwards, trembling slightly.

"I never expected that," he said, quite obviously shaken.

"What happened?" Alyssa asked.

"Your magic was greater than I had planned. I didn't expect it, and couldn't control it. It began to dominate mine."

"So I have some magic?"

The Unicorn started intently at her, as though seeing her for the first time. "Yes,' he said slowly. "You have magic. It doesn't make any sense. You have no training; no particular discipline and you come from a world that is very weak in magic. And yet you have more pure, untrained magic than any creature I have ever felt.

"Even the greatest wizard could never hope to compare to you!"

CHAPTER THREE

Magic in the Mountains

"But will it be enough to get us back home?" Alyssa asked, infused with sudden hope. "I mean, along with the Norf's magic."

"I can't guarantee that," Blue replied thoughtfully. "Only the Norfs will know. Without question, they can harmonize with you and use your power. Anyone with training—that you allow—can do this. Even I can, for battle and defense—my discipline. However, that is something that you must now think about. Even though you might not be able to use it, such a great magic would be an incredible asset in our current war. You could help Tanzal a great deal."

"I don't want to fight in wars," Alyssa replied quietly. "I just want to go home. You don't understand, if we don't make it home tonight, our parents are gonna freak. We'll be the lead story come six-o'clock news time. Brett and I'll be on mailers and posters across America inside a week. My mom wigs over kidnappings. It's her biggest fear."

Blue nodded in resignation. "I don't fully understand everything you just said, but I do understand the sentiment. Tanzal's problems are not yours. And I agree, you must be returned to your parents."

The unicorn glanced around himself as though looking for something. He apparently didn't spy it, and so turned back toward them. He took two steps forward and then knelt down. "It is a long trip to the home of the Norfs. You shall have to ride or it would take us far too long."

"We won't fall off, will we?" Alyssa asked, stepping forward cautiously. She reached out and touched his mane. It was as soft as goose down.

"Trust me, you will *not* fall off. Nothing on Tanzal could ride a unicorn if the unicorn didn't wish it. But no rider that has been given the privilege of being bourne by one of us has *ever* fallen. We tolerate no saddle, bridle or bit—a unicorn would rather die first. And I truly mean that. But you are safer on my bare back than if you were strapped into the saddle of a horse, even a talking one with magic. Now up you go. We have a long trip if we are to make camp in the Rockroller Mountains tonight at the Norf's cave."

Brett and Alyssa climbed carefully on. Blue's back was softer and more comfortable than a padded saddle. Alyssa took the front, twining her hands in his mane, while Brett wrapped his arms around his big sister. The unicorn stood up smoothly. It seemed to take no effort at all. A sense of pure, animal strength seemed to flow from him. At first, he walked, letting them get used to the feel of being on his back. But then Blue quickly picked up the pace, first a trot, then a gallop, and finally, a full out run that sent them across the meadow like the wind.

The ground beneath them was little more than a blur, the forest beside them not much more.

"This is *sooo* cool," Brett whispered in Alyssa's ear. She didn't answer him. She had been allowed to run Katie's horse once on the round track at Herriman city's W. And M. Butterfield rodeo grounds, but it had been nothing like this. That had simply been running on a horse, kind of exciting but more than a little scary. This felt more like flying on a magic carpet. And Blue was right. She never once felt as if she might fall. It was magic.

It didn't take long before they came to the end of the meadow, a place where the forest met the sea, and Blue had to slow his pace as he took a trail between the trees. After a while, the path veered sharply to the right and began to climb. The unicorn now slowed to a walk as he picked his way along the rocky trail.

"We are climbing the South Sea Mountains," he informed them. "They're really more like hills. It won't take us long."

For almost an hour they climbed through the thin timber, the trail winding and turning but always heading north. In one of the trees, Alyssa spied two of the large, quiet squirrels like the one she had seen near the meadow. Blue nodded to them as he passed. She also saw dozens of regular squirrels—small, scolding and scampering among the pines. Bright blue flowers bloomed in profusion in the sunnier spots—they looked like a combination between a bluebell and a honeysuckle and covered the earth like blue shag carpet—while long grass grew almost everywhere else. Small, yellow butterflies and black bees flew among the flowers.

The trail began to gently flatten as they approached the crest of the hills. When they reached the top, Blue stopped for a minute. His breathing was even and light, as though he had made hardly any effort at all so far, and his fur shone with only a light glint of sweat.

"We have reached the Kaparowitzs valley," he said. "You may wish to take a small break now. The road ahead is wide and flat and made of soft earth. Once we are on it, I shall not stop or even slow down, and you shall see the true speed of a unicorn. Nothing on Tanzal can match us. Which is why we are the Queen's couriers as well as her personal guard."

"You weren't going as fast as you could when we were down in the meadow?" Brett asked in amazement.

Blue laughed lightly. "No, my dear boy," he said. "I'm afraid not. I had too pick my way through the South Sea Meadow. It is the only place that the Meadow Tigers grow, and they are protected by law as well as magic. Grazing is not even allowed, and it would be a tragedy if I stepped on one, so I watched carefully as I ran. Now, if you wish a break, you can jump down."

"I'm fine," Brett said happily.

Alyssa shifted on the unicorn's back, testing her muscles. Her legs weren't really all that cramped and she was more than a little impatient to reach the Norf's and get sent back home. She could take a break then.

"I'm fine, too," she said.

"Good enough," the unicorn replied as he stepped out again, breaking into a trot.

The trail rapidly flattened and grew wide. The gently rolling hills around them were covered with tall grass and stands of trees that looked like aspens and birches. They stretched away into the distance for as far as Alyssa could see. Blue now began to run again. But this time—as unbelievable as it was—he ran even faster than before. His legs were nothing but a blur of speed. The earth flew by beneath them like magic. The wind whipped Alyssa's hair and stung her eyes. She had never flown in a open plane before, but she imagined that it was something like this. She leaned forward and hid her face in the unicorn's mane, while she felt Brett hiding his in the back of her shirt.

After a while, the gentle rhythm of the unicorn's running coupled with the warmth from his neck, made Alyssa start to doze. Back at home, it would have been evening by now, while here the sun was just reaching its zenith; it was going to be a very long day.

Juxtaposition lag, Alyssa thought wryly to herself.

But even though she dozed on and off throughout that afternoon, she never once felt as if she were going to fall off. It was as though she were being cradled on his back.

As they ran the hills around them changed little, but sometimes, when she glanced up, Alyssa spied herds of animals grazing in the distance. They were too far away to tell exactly what they were, but they looked a combination between a cow and a buffalo.

With a sudden start, Alyssa woke to find that Blue was slowing down. She looked up and found the sun hanging low in the western sky, and tall, rocky mountains rising directly in front of them. Their steep slopes were covered with huge boulders, oakbrush and stunted pines. They began to climb a rocky, barren trail up the mountainside. It wound back and forth and then dived into a narrow canyon. The canyon's walls were sheer rock and almost completely devoid of plant life. Only a few struggling clumps of grass grew alongside the trail.

"This is home of the Norf's," Blue said quietly. "I have only been here twice before, both times on the Queen's business. They aren't really very friendly, and the Rockroller Mountains aren't the kind of place one wants to stay in for long."

As they followed the canyon farther in, the trail flattened and the canyon walls grew farther apart. A few stunted cedars dotted the widening valley floor.

"Illsonian de Allgrath!" Alyssa heard a high voice crying off to her right. She turned to see a small, gnarled man standing on a nearby boulder. He was at the very most three feet tall and dressed in a white flowing robe. In his right hand he held a wooden wand, which he waved in a circle in the air above his head.

"Seal it now!" he cried and jumped down from the stone as spryly as an imp of the devil. The little man then turned toward them and smiled mischievously. "We've been watching your coming for hours now, Blue, and have been waiting impatiently for you to arrive. Come, and enjoy the warmth of our fire!"

He then laughed as if this were a great joke and disappeared into a maze of boulders behind him.

Blue stamped his hoof in irritation. He looked back at the trail they had just ridden up and muttered something under his breath. Several small blue sparkles floated in the air around his head.

"I don't understand this at all. He has cast a very powerful containing spell. It follows behind us and would take a great effort for me to break. We can only go forward. He shouldn't have done this." The unicorn turned back. His voice was hard and grim as he continued. "I was going to have you walk from here, but now I think you should stay on my back. Come, let us go and see what mischief our little gnomish friends are up to."

"Was that one of the Norfs?" Alyssa asked.

"Yes," the unicorn replied as he picked his way up the valley. "It was Ballus, the youngest of the three brothers. He uses a wand for magic. Reemus is the middle brother, and the warrior of the three. He carries a sword. Atticus is the oldest and strongest, in fact the only one with true power. He needs none of those things. His magic comes from his hands. I fear that something has gone terribly wrong for them to have the audacity to cast spells at the Queen's couriers. But if they think that they can harass me at this time, they are making a grave mistake! I know something that they don't know!"

The trail turned now and wound to the left, weaving between the gnarled trees and heading toward a sheer rock cliff. At the base of the cliff, Alyssa could see a small fire burning in front of a large cave. Three small figures stood around it.

"What is the meaning of your spell?" Blue demanded as he approached the fire. "Why have you contained us?"

The middle of the three men turned and stared at the visitors. He was also dressed in a long, flowing white robe that hung to ground and hid his hands in their folds. His face was pale white and his skin was wrinkled and old, like dried leather that has been left in the sun too long. But the old Norf's eyes were a dark, navy blue, and fairly danced with an excited light. His voice dripped with contempt when he spoke.

"How long have you been down there, all alone and watching the Juxtaposition, my dear Blue Unicorn?" he asked. "Thirty days? Thirty-five? We first noticed you at the South Sea Meadow three weeks ago. You have been out of contact for far too long. So much has changed since you went away!"

Blue snorted. "So much that you would dare insult one of the Queen's Unicorns—which has come to you seeking aid? So much that you would try to contain me with a following spell?"

The third brother, who was the tallest of the three and carried a sword in a scabbard across his back, laughed out loud. It sounded more like a cackle than a laugh.

"Who can blame the spider when the fly comes of its own accord? And how many centuries has it been since we had a good unicorn steak? I have no idea, but I know for a fact that we've never eaten a Blue one! We shall dine like kings tonight, with humans for desert!"

He then reached onto his back and drew his sword. It was short and bright, and its razorlike edge glinted in the last of the setting sun's rays. All three of the Norf's robes began to glisten and sparkle with silvery lights.

"You will do no such thing," Blue stated flatly. His voice was grim and hard. He seemed to suddenly grow, infused with power.

"The Wizarding Council has bound you from such evil. But even so, beware for not only am I a Blue Unicorn, but I am also a keeper of the secret Flame of Andwar and a Captain in its brotherhood. You threaten me at your own great peril!"

"Oh, my foolish unicorn!" the center brother cried, lifting his hands above his head. His gnarled fingers glowed with light. "Have you seeken the Flame of Andwar of late? Have you tried to draw from its power? I think not. The Wizarding Council is broken! Its binding is gone. And I now draw power from a dark source long kept from me. For you see, the Great Northern Shield had been destroyed completely! Seek now the Flame of Andwar, and you shall see I speak the truth. The Chief of Andwar is dead, and the Brotherhood Of The Unicorn is decimated! Many of its members have been killed in battle, and its flame, once a roaring torch, is now naught but a flickering candle in a growing storm!

"And I shall have the great privilege of diminishing that flame even further by destroying you!"

The Norfs hands suddenly flashed with lightening and the air was filled with silvery, spinning magic lights. They swarmed toward them, spinning wildly, followed by Reemus and his sword. Blue snorted and lowered his head. His blue magic lights appeared around him, and his horn glowed with a white light. He stamped the rock in front of him. It shattered in a shower of sparks. He then reared and pawed the air. His hooves shone with silver fire.

When he came down, he crossed his horn with Reemus' sword and they began to duel.

But Reemus drove him slowly backward, his sword a blur of flashing light. And Atticus' magic lights grew stronger and wilder, while Blue's grew slower and fainter. The unicorn backed up a step at a time, until he hit the containment spell. He could go no further, and his magic was almost destroyed.

Reemus' sword flicked his front shoulder. It drew a line of blood.

Put your hands on my neck! a voice spoke inside Alyssa's head. *Open yourself to me. The flame of Andwar is all but gone. Let me draw from you!*

Alyssa grabbed Blue's neck. She closed her eyes and concentrated on him. A tingle ran up her arms. It felt as if something were being pulled out of her. It was at first a trickle, but it quickly turned into a stream—and then a rushing torrent! Feeling lightheaded, almost like she was hypnotized, she opened her eyes to find Blue's magic lights were now a raging whirlwind of power. They spun in a storm all around the small clearing, clashing with the Norfs'. Blue on silver. Silver on blue. They were so thick that she could see almost nothing else.

And, slowly but surely, Blue's magic-lights grew stronger and stronger driving the Norf's silvery magic-lights backwards in the same fashion that they had at first driven his.

Then with renewed strength and speed, Blue attacked Reemus' defenses. His horn flashed and flew, parried and thrust. Now, Reemus was forced to take a step back—first one, then another, and then another. His face showed surprise, and sudden concern. It wasn't supposed to happen like this! No unicorn should be this strong!

Blue drove the Norf slowly back to his fire and the edge of the cliff.

Suddenly, a finger of Blue's magic-lights broke off and slammed into the side of the cliff. A shower of stones sprayed down on the three Norfs. It caused Reemus' defense to falter, and Blue took advantage of the opening by rushing forward and driving his horn through the little man. He lifted him completely off the ground. Reemus' sword clattered onto the rocks. Blue shook his head and threw him. The warrior Norf landed in a lifeless heap beside the fire.

The Unicorn reared again, neighing triumphantly. Flames leapt from his hooves. When he came down, the earth shook beneath him, rumbling like an earthquake. Rocks fell from the cliffs all around them. Blue's magic lights now went completely wild, driving the Norf's backward in sudden, overpowering rush.

Then, in a flash, it was all over. All the lights suddenly disappeared, and the two remaining Norfs cowered before them.

"You have been beaten!" Blue cried loudly. "Do you seek

quarter?"

But before they could answer, the air was filled with red magic lights and a strong voice spoke behind them.

"Sitoneim al Ent!" the voice cried loudly. "Stone hold you until judgment!"

Then the air flashed with more red magic and the two remaining Norfs turned into glistening, white marble.

Blue whirled around. Standing in front of them was a tall lady, dressed all in red and holding a golden wand.

"Your majesty!" Blue exclaimed. "How are you here?"

"I am ghosting," she replied. Alyssa now noticed that she could see through the woman. She was indeed a faint, floating figure. "It is costing me precious power. But when I felt a great magic being used here, I had to come. Blue, the Wizarding Council has suffered a treachery beyond words. They were betrayed by two of their members, and all but three are dead. The two traitors—the dark leader Lord Falgerth and his liege Lord Layton—in league with the Norfs have brought down the Great Northern Shield, and attacked Tanzal with an army out of the north. They march on Altian even as we speak, driving the remnants of my unicorn guard and the last of our northern defenders in front of them. Here in Altian, we prepare for battle and siege.

"Blue, you must listen carefully. I haven't much time left. My power fades and draws me back. The Ancient One secretly prophesied about this day, and with his last act of magic, he made it so that his vast power would return and rebuild his shield if it ever failed. He said that his magic would be revealed with a blow grievous to Tanzal's enemies, and turn the tides of war. And so it has! The Norfs dark powers had grown immense with the destruction of the shield but they are now no more. They are encased in Judgment Stone, and standing here, I now see the truth. The Ancient One's power has indeed returned at the fall of his great shield, just as he said.

"Blue, the Ancient One's magic resides in that young girl who is sitting on your back!"

CHAPTER FOUR

Treasure Cave

"But now you must listen closely, Blue," the queen continued urgently. "My time grows short. Raspal is at Tiernan village. I shall send him with supplies and a guard. You must meet him at the confluence of the Starlight and Terry rivers by tomorrow night. You will have to carry the children and run all day in order to make it.

"Blue, it is essential that they be under guard as soon as possible. I am sure that Lord Falgerth has also sensed this magic. And I am absolutely positive that he knows by now that the one of the Norf's is dead and the other two are in my stone, awaiting judgment. He has lost a major battle here tonight. It is his first loss, and so a very painful one. Remember, he will come after you, and not the children. You drew her power, and made it yours. Until I probed her just now, even I thought that it was your magic at work—that you had somehow come by the Ancient One's power. Be on your guard and do not let Lord Falgerth probe you or the girl. I, and the remaining wizards from the Council, will Shield her as best we can from afar.

"Above all else, Blue, keep her safe! She is all that stands between us and destruction!"

Alyssa had been listening to all this with a growing sense of unease. She had told Blue that she didn't want to fight in the Tanzal's wars, and yet in her first day with him, she had been threatened with being eaten, taken part in a battle, watched a small man killed and two more turned to stone, and was now part of a plot to rebuild some kind of shield.

Summoning all her courage, she asked timidly, "But how are Brett and I going to get home to our world? We're really not soldiers. We can't fight wars."

The Queen turned her gaze to Alyssa. Her outline was beginning to noticeably fade. She smiled apologetically. "I'm sorry, child, I haven't even asked your name. My time is so short. But let me assure you that as long as the Ancient One's power lies in you, you will stay in Tanzal. It is Tanzal's magic. She will not let it go. You must make your way to Spellcasting Peak in the Impassable Mountains where I beleive his magic will take over and rebuild the Great Northern Shield. I am not sure, but I believe your being here is also part of the spell. Once you rebuild the Shield, I think that you and your brother will be returned to your own world. At least, that is my hope. We will do our best to protect you and help you while you are still here in Tanzal.

"But my power fades. You are one of the few remaining Unicorns of Andwar, Blue, and also the Blue Unicorn. I think you see your Quest before you! Remember to keep them shielded at all times! And beware of Lord Falgerth!"

And then, in a flash of red magic lights, the Queen was gone. The unicorn took a deep breath and lowered his head. He stared at the ground for a long minute. A slight shiver ran though his body and Alyssa saw a tear drip onto the ground.

"You must get down," he said quietly. "I am weary. My father was the Chief of Andwar, and now he is passed. The Brotherhood of the Unicorn is decimated and my older brother has not been able to reform it without me. Black times are indeed upon us. War is a horrible thing."

The unicorn knelt gently, and Alyssa and Brett slipped off. Alyssa didn't know what to do or say and so simply stood by the fire, while Blue gazed down at the ground. His eyes were clouded and sad, his head was bent and his spirit seemed broken. Brett found the Norf's woodpile and threw a couple of large logs on the small campfire. They caught quickly and the dancing flames kept back the deepening twilight. He then walked over to the two marble statues and cautiously felt them. They glistened in the growing firelight.

"Cool," he said in awe. "How long will they stay like this?"

"Until the Queen lets them out for judgment," Blue said, glancing up. "Her spell was cast with no defense on their part. They were completely beaten by Alyssa's magic—which makes the charm so strong that only the Queen herself can break it. If something happens to her, or if she decides to leave them like that, they will stay in stone forever."

The unicorn then bent his head and using his horn speared a corner of the dead Norf's robe. He lifted him off the ground.

"I shall take care of this," he stated flatly and disappeared into the dark.

When Blue returned about a half-hour later, his head was again erect and proud and his step and stance were firmer, more resolute.

"Well, children," he said. "The times we live in are not for us to choose, nor are the Quests that are laid before us. We can only do the best that we can, and what will be, will be. Wouldn't you agree, Alyssa?"

"I don't know," she stuttered. "I really don't understand what's going on. How did this "Ancient One's" power come to me? And why can't I just get rid of it and go home? Who is he anyways?"

"These are all good questions," Blue answered gravely. "And I will try my best to answer them. How you came by the Ancient One's power is beyond my knowledge, but who he was, is not.

"The Legends say that the Ancient One's real name was Kolvard Newhand. He was born in Cliffland in the far north of Tanzal many ages ago, where he is still known as Kolvard The Old or Kolvard the Wise. The rest of Tanzal call him either The Ancient One or The Guardian.

"When Kolvard was young, it was discovered that he had a great, natural magic—one of the greatest ever seen. His training and natural discipline was Shielding, and he spent his entire life learning about it and perfecting his art. In his lifetime, Tanzal was not as you see her now. Back then, she was torn by the Dark Wars between her good and evil sides. Her Southern end is the source of her Light

Magic, and her Northern end is the source of her Black Magic, and until Kolvard's day, they had always been at war with each other. In his lifetime, Kolvard became a Great Mage and fighter in the Dark Wars. Many of his shields were so powerful that they protected entire armies of men and unicorns, making them virtually indestructible. He also formed the first Wizarding Council and became its leader, and together with Tanzal's first crowned King, they drove much that was dark into the far north of Tanzal.

"But The Guardian's greatest achievement came near the end of his long life. He knew that once he was gone, and with him his great shields, war and darkness would return to Tanzal. The legends say that he and the Wizarding Council spent his last few years casting some of the greatest magic ever seen into three large Tanzalite stones—the Guardian Stones—and then, at the end of his days, Kolvard Newhand took these stones and climbed a mountain at the far end of Cliffland now known as Spellcasting Peak. There he created his greatest shield of all. The weaving of this vast spell took several days, and during it, all of Tanzal lay under the shine of its casting.

"When he was finally done, Kolvard Newhand had created The Great Northern Shield, and then he passed. His final and greatest shield split Tanzal into two sides, one side dark, one side light, and prevented any magic from passing between the two.

"In time, the dark, Northern side became a vast, ruinous wasteland, where very few things live and even less that is green grows, while her Southern side became as you see it now, beautiful and free and a place where what little Black Magic there is, is weak and cannot stand in the face of our powerful Light Magic."

At this, the unicorn stopped talking, bowed his head and sighed. Finally, he glanced up and finished.

"But now, I'm afraid that Kolvard's Shield is indeed gone, and dark times are upon us again if we cannot fix it. I am also afraid that the Queen is right. If indeed the magic in you is The Ancient One's, then you will not be allowed to return to your world unless you cast it from yourself at the top of Spellcasting Peak. Whether or not you can rebuild the shield probably, for you, doesn't matter, but you must try. Either way, whether you succeed or fail, the magic will be gone and you will probably return to your own world. Does this answer your questions, child?"

"I guess," Alyssa replied. "But I still don't understand it all. I mean, why is Brett here? What does he have to do with anything? He doesn't have any magic."

"You are right," Blue said, nodding with understanding. "Not everything in this matter is clear, even to our Wise. I think that in time, we will understand. But now, come and let's see what our little friends, the Norfs, house is like. I'm sure that we will be the first to see the inside of it in an age. I wonder what they've managed to squirrel away over the years. I don't doubt but that it's a great deal of stuff, and I know that they love jewels. At the very least we shall find beds for you tonight."

"And a bathroom too, maybe?" Alyssa asked timidly.

"Of course," Blue replied. "Here, Brett, take a stick and light it in the fire. We'll use it to light what torches or candles we find. I'm sure they have some."

The cave entrance was high enough for the unicorn to walk in unbent, about eight feet tall, and just inside it a few steps, they found two swinging doors. They were ornately carved and made of a dark, oily-looking wood. They weren't locked and swung easily open when Brett pulled. Inside, several tall white candles burned in holders on the wall of a large, open living room. The ceiling of the cave was covered with a mirror-like glass, which reflected the light brightly—it was almost like electric lights at home. Brett snubbed out his burning stick. There was no point to keeping it lit.

The tables in the room—three of them, a kitchen table and two other smaller ones—were carved out of solid, black stone. They were embedded with a great many green gemstones that looked like uncut emeralds. Against one of the kitchen walls stood a series of beautifully carved wood cabinets with an immaculate green-marble washbasin at the end.

In the living room portion of this great room, there were three small, cloth-covered chairs in front of the coffee tables. Two of its walls had floor to ceiling bookshelves, which were filled with old, leather-bound tomes. The entire floor was made of a closely-fitted, grey shale stone, and everything was spotless.

Alyssa gazed around in awe. This wasn't like any cave she'd ever been in! She now noticed that the exposed, flat rock walls were embedded with a variety of cut stones. Some were small and gemlike, while others were larger and multicolored. Several had veins of what looked like pure gold running through them.

Blue stepped purposefully toward a stone hallway at the far end of the room. He had to duck his head and horn to enter. Brett and Alyssa followed. Several candles burned in holders along its length. They came to another chamber at the far end. It contained two more of the black tables, three more chairs, another bookshelf, and three small beds lined against the wall. Each bed had a single pillow and were piled high with the tanned furs of a white-haired animal.

"I believe that is the bathroom," Blue said, nodding toward a small door on the right. Alyssa opened it and peered in cautiously. It had a small stone tub and toilet basin. Both had streams of water trickling through them. She was relieved to see a stack of soft papers next to the toilet. After closing the door, Alyssa took a large handful of them and stuffed them into her back pocket—for future use—and then thought about it, and filled her front pocket as well. The pile remained the exact same size.

When Alyssa came out of the bathroom, she found both Brett and the unicorn staring at the only empty wall in the room.

"Blue says it's another room, probably a storeroom," Brett explained. "It's got a hidden entrance. He's trying to break it open magically."

It looked like any of the other rock walls to Alyssa. The unicorn muttered something under his breath, shook his horn, and blue magic-lights appeared. Nothing happened. He did this several more times, but got nowhere.

"It's too strong for me," he finally admitted. "I don't even think that the spell can be broken. I think that we shall have to break the door itself." He turned to Alyssa. "I need to borrow your magic again. I hate to do it; it will take so much that anyone tuned to the lines of power will instantly know about it. Lord Falgerth will sense me a second time, and the Queen will wonder what has happened. But I think we have no choice. Something very important is in there. I feel it in my bones. Put your hand on my shoulder and open your mind to me."

Alyssa did as she was asked, and she closed her eyes to concentrate. The first time Blue had drawn her power had been in the chaos of a battle, and she had had no idea what was going on. This time, however, it was a calm and quiet experience. First her hand, and then her entire arm tingled intensely. She fell into a sudden trancelike state as the magic was pulled from her. It felt as though Blue was taking only a small cupful out of what was a large lake. She seemed to be floating on air. In a daze, she opened her eyes to find the room filled with wildly spinning blue magic-lights.

"*Obrese eh Circom!*" the unicorn cried. He reared and hit the wall with one of his front hooves. A small crack appeared where he struck it. It quickly spider webbed out in all directions. A four-foot by four-foot section of the wall suddenly crumbled into a pile of gravel, revealing a small room behind it.

"Cool," Brett said in awe. "I wish I could do that! That kicks butt!"

As the dust cleared, Alyssa peered curiously in. The storeroom was a small circular cave, about eight feet wide, ten feet deep and only four feet high. It contained two dark, wooden chests, a large leather sack, several bows with arrows, and a sword in a scabbard hanging on the wall.

"I'm too tall," Blue said. "Take a candle, Brett, and go see what's in those chests."

"Is it safe?" Alyssa asked with excitement. "Can I go too?"

The unicorn nodded. "Go ahead. I think it's safe enough. The only magic I sense is the spell holding the door locked. But that's not a problem because the door isn't there anymore."

Brett grabbed a candle and the two kids scrambled in. He quickly opened the closest chest and it was just as Alyssa had thought—it was full of treasure; gold coins in fact. They sparkled brightly in the candlelight. The second chest contained more, as well as some silver ones. Alyssa picked up a handful of them. They were about the size of silver dollars and they were rough and uneven, not at all like the smooth, perfectly round American coins that she was used to. Some had pictures of men on the front, others women, all of which looked like Kings and Queens. Most had scenes of mountains on the back, although one had a large lake and another a pair of flying eagles. She dropped them back into the chest and watched as Brett untied the rope from around the leather sack. He pulled it free and upended the bag.

A stream of jewels poured out onto the cave floor in a huge pile. They were the colors of the rainbow. Red rubies, blue sapphires, green emeralds, yellow topaz, white diamonds. And they were all shapes and sizes. A light green stone caught Alyssa's eye and she picked it up. It was a fully round stone, intricately cut on all sides and about the size of a very large marble. It was probably an emerald, but sparkled in the candlelight like an incredible diamond. She found another just like it and rolled them around in her palm. This was a fortune, she marveled to herself as stared at them all. Even the Smithsonian didn't have this many gems!

"Are these all the Norf's?" Alyssa asked. "Or did they steal them from other people, like pirates do."

"I can't say for sure. Probably a little of both. All I'm positive about is that they're ours now. The Norfs will be lucky to get their lives returned to them, much less anything else. Now, Brett, please bring me that sword. I'm curious about it."

Brett lifted the sword from its peg on the wall. He carried it carefully across the pile of rubble and held it out for Blue's inspection. The unicorn stared at it intently. Its handle and guard were made of plain steel, smooth and simple. Its only decoration was a single dark green gemstone the size of a golf ball embedded in the tip of its handle.

"Please draw it for me," Blue said quietly. Brett pulled it from its leather scabbard

"Oh, awesome!" he exclaimed. "It makes my arm tingle, like electricity!"

The blade of the sword glistened brightly. It looked razor sharp. And for an instant, gold ruins shone on its side, running up and down like thin lines of written flame.

"I believe this is the Sword of Cabral," Blue said. "It's long been rumored that the Gnomes, not the Norfs, had regained it. Historically, it was actually first the Gnomes, but stolen from them long ago. They commissioned it's creation from the Elves, and it's forged in deep Elvish magic. I think you should keep it, Brett, until you return to your world. It should help keep you safe. It's said to defend its possessor. If Reemus had wielded this blade today, things might have turned out very differently. Luckily for us, he didn't think he needed it."

"If Brett gets that sword, can I keep these jewels?" Alyssa asked, holding out the two, light-green stones that she had picked up.

"Of course," Blue replied. "But you know that they won't return with you to your world. You may only have them while you're here in Tanzal. Both of you should also take a few of the gold talents. They might come in useful.

"Now, Alyssa, there is something else in this room. I can feel it. It has a strong presence. Walk to the back and feel along the wall, just above your head. Something is hidden there."

Alyssa did as he asked. At first, she felt nothing—only blank rock wall. It was smooth and cold. Then her hands ran across an invisible outcropping; it was the strangest sensation she'd ever had. Her hands were feeling something square and hard and very real, but her eyes saw nothing but air between her fingers! She pushed and pulled at the invisible box, but it refused to budge.

Then, suddenly, her fingers stuck to its sides like they were glued, and she felt magic being pulled from her. The box began to quiver and shake as if some small animal were inside trying to get free. There was a loud *"POP"*, like a light bulb going out, and her hands were pushed forcefully away.

Alyssa jumped backwards in surprise. Something square and brown fell to the cave floor with a loud *thump!*

"Bring it to me," Blue said.

"I am *not* touching that!" Alyssa stated emphatically. "Whatever it is, it's alive. And it can stay right there for all I care."

"Will you bring it to me, Brett?" Blue sounded a bit annoyed.

"Sure, whatever," Brett replied "I ain't scared of it." He eagerly set down his sword and scrambled over the gravel pile. Despite his bravado, he approached the thing cautiously. Alyssa stepped back even further as Brett bent to look at it. He reached down and picked it up.

"It's just an old book, you big wimp," he said with a laugh. "It's not alive."

"You didn't feel it when it was trying to get out," Alyssa retorted. "It *felt* like it was alive. *You* don't have any magic in you. You don't know how weird it is."

"Yeah, yeah, yeah," Brett said as he walked by her. "Everything's always so tough. Poor little Lyssa."

Alyssa gritted her teeth and followed Brett out of the storeroom. He could be such a pain in the rear. Mr. Know It All.

In the light of the bedroom, she could see that it was indeed only a book—a very old one. It was bound in brown leather with raised white lettering. The writing was a flowing cursive that looked like some strange, cryptic language. The words almost looked like ruins. It wasn't a very thick book, with maybe only a half-inch of yellowed papers showing between the covers. A small lock—like the one on Alyssa's diary at home—latched the back cover to the front. Brett held it out for the unicorn to inspect.

"This is a very strange find," he said slowly. His voice held a note of awe. "I have only seen three other books like this before. The Wizarding Council holds them in their council room in Castle Tiernan. They are the three *Books of Magic*, written by the Ancient One at the height of his power. Legend has it that he wrote a fourth book—a much smaller one—as the end of his life neared. No one knows what it is about. No one has ever read it. That lock may look small, but I think the magic it would take to open it hasn't been seen on Tanzal since his death.

"Unless I'm gravely mistaken, this is the legendary *Fourth Book of Magic.*"

"What'll we do with it?" Brett asked.

"We'll take it with us, of course," Blue replied. "I don't think it's at all a coincidence that the Ancient One's magic and his *Fourth Book* both reappear on the same day. Alyssa was meant to find it."

"I don't want it," Alyssa said shaking her head. She could feel herself stressing out. This was all getting just a little too weird. "I'm not touching it again. It gives me the creeps just to look at it. I didn't ask to have magic, and I don't want any magic book."

The unicorn nodded. "I understand," he said. "This has been a very long day for you, and you are young. Rest will help you. It is time for sleep. Will you carry the book as well as your sword, Brett? I will feel better if you sleep out by the fire, where I can watch you while I graze. Perhaps you should grab some blankets, Alyssa, and throw them over me. I promise you that they're not magical."

"Don't you need to sleep?" Brett asked.

"I do," Blue answered. "But not like humans do. I require only a couple of hours a night, even after my great run today. A patch of good grass is more important. I haven't eaten all day, and I'm as hungry as a horse!"

The unicorn chuckled at his little joke—he seemed extremely amused by it—as Alyssa lifted several of the Norf's white, sleeping furs onto his back. Like everything else the Norf's owned, they were very clean, as well as soft. You could call the little men a lot of other things, Alyssa thought, but you couldn't call them messy housekeepers.

The three of them trooped back out to the fire, where Alyssa arranged the furs while Brett threw a couple of logs on. It had died down while they were gone, but he had it roaring again in no time.

"I saw a nice patch of grass over near those trees," Blue said, nodding to the north. "I'll be just a few feet away. Yell if you need anything, or if anything bothers you."

"You don't think that there's something around here for us to eat, do you?" Brett asked. "I'm kinda hungry too. We haven't eaten anything all day."

"Oh, dear me, of course," Blue said. "What am I thinking? Try in the Norf's kitchen, Brett. I'm sure they have something. But perhaps you shouldn't eat any of the meat you find there, just to be on the safe side."

"Yeah. I gotcha on that one," Brett said, chuckling. He muttered something about *people jerky* as he walked back to the cave. Blue trotted off into the darkness, leaving Alyssa alone by the fire. She settled onto her furs and sighed.

They weren't going to make it home tonight; that was for sure. In fact, it didn't look like they were going to make it home anytime soon—if ever. Their parents, especially their mom, were going to panic completely. Alyssa started to lightly cry. She felt horrible for her mom now that it was nighttime. She probably had the entire neighborhood, not to mention most of the Sandy Police force, out looking for them in the dark. Everyone was probably blaming her, because she was the oldest. But, dang it, it wasn't her fault! She hadn't meant for this to happen, and she was doing everything she could to get home!

Alyssa heard Brett opening the cave doors again and so dried her eyes. She didn't want him to see her crying. He'd probably make fun of her. He was quite obviously having a good time here. This was an adventure—right up his alley.

"We're in luck, Lyssa, I found some bread and butter, and some funny looking, red fruit." He sat down next to her and showed her a round melon about the size and texture of a small cantaloupe but bright red, like an apple. He dropped it into her lap and then tore off a piece of bread from a large, oval loaf. Brett smothered this with a runny, butter like spread that he scooped from a wooden bowl, and took a big bite.

"Ah, man, that's good!" he exclaimed. He tore off another piece and smothered it for her. "You gotta try this, Lyssa. That's the best bread and honey-butter I've ever had. I'll bet it's magic. Everything here is."

Alyssa reluctantly took the bread. She wasn't all that excited to eat strange food found in some strange little men's cupboard, but she was also extremely hungry. She took a small bite. The honey butter spread was perhaps the sweetest and creamiest thing she'd ever tasted, and the bread was soft and fresh. Okay, she admitted to herself as she quickly ate the entire piece, there was nothing wrong with this.

The two of them ate for fifteen minutes straight, finishing off the entire loaf and most of the honey-butter. Brett then pulled out his scout knife and cut the fruit in half. The melon's flesh was dark green, the color of pine needles, with yellow seeds in the center. He cleaned out the seeds with his small spoon and handed her half of it.

"You first this time," he said, holding out the spoon.

"No," Alyssa said. "I'm not going first. Ever. You're Mr. Adventure. You go first."

Brett shrugged his shoulders. "Okay," he said. "Why not." He ate a large spoonful, and grimaced. "It's kinda bitter. I don't think I like it."

"Well, I definitely don't want any then. I'm full enough."

Brett set the melon aside and threw a couple more logs on the already roaring fire.

"Do you think you should do that?" Alyssa asked. "Shouldn't we save some of the firewood?"

"For what? Tomorrow? I think we're leaving early in the morning, from the sounds of it. And I doubt we're coming back here." Brett threw on another log. "Might as well have a deer-hunting fire. You've never seen one of those; they're big."

Alyssa didn't argue. He was right. But nevertheless, the large fire made her uncomfortable. Someone—or something—might see it and come to investigate. She slid her furs back; it was getting too hot.

"Mom's gonna be freaking out about now," she said quietly.

"I know," Brett replied, his tone serious for the first time that day. "I've thought about that. I'm sure Dad's fine, but Mom's probably crying her eyes out. But what do we do about that, Alyssa? What can we do? It's not like we ran away from home. It's more like this planet kidnapped us. It's not our fault. We just get home as fast as we can, and then everything will be okay."

Alyssa didn't answer. He was right again, and at least he seemed to actually care about someone other than himself. She lied down, wrapped herself in her furs and stared up at the strange stars and constellations above her. They *were* going to get home, she told herself. They were. It was just going to take a little time. The large meal began to make her drowsy, and she slowly slipped into sleep.

Only Brett was awake when Tanzal's three large, full moons rose—they formed a triangle in the sky.

CHAPTER FIVE

In the Company of Wolves

Alyssa woke in the morning from a gentle nudge to her side, and she opened her eyes to find Blue standing above her. The sun was still behind the mountains but the sky was bright with a growing dawn. The unicorn stepped over and nudged Brett awake.

"I let you sleep as long as I could. But it is time to get going. I have a long run ahead of me today. Here, Brett, I got this for you."

The unicorn dropped a leather back scabbard from his horn. Brett crawled out of his furs and tried it on—it fit him perfectly, and held his sword tight across his back and out of the way. Alyssa thought it looked suspiciously like the one that Reemus had been wearing, but didn't say anything. It also looked a little wet, like maybe Blue had cleaned it up. She wouldn't wear that thing for all the gold in Egypt and all the tea in China put together, she decided. But Brett looked as pleased as punch.

"Cool," he said as he reached onto his back and pulled his sword free, and then slipped it easily back in. He did this several times for practice, and each time the blade came out, the gold ruins on its silver side flickered up and down. "I like it."

"Go and fetch some breakfast for the two of you, Brett. We must be going. We have a long day of travel ahead of us if we are to make it to the Starfire River by tonight. Raspal will be waiting, I'm sure. He only has a couple of hours of travel from Tiernan Village."

Brett scampered into the Norf's cave and returned with another loaf of bread and bowl of honey-butter. He also had found a bag full of what looked like biscuits. The two of them ate a quick breakfast while the unicorn scooped up the furs and set them just inside the cave. He then said something under his breath and a few, small blue magic-lights flickered in the air.

"Not much of a Binding Spell. But at least it will keep the animals and curiosity seekers out. A real magician would have no trouble in breaking it. Now up you go."

Blue knelt down and Alyssa scrambled up. Brett followed carrying the bag of biscuits and the *Fourth Book of Magic*. He set it between them as he wrapped his arms around her waist. It seemed to quiver the slightest bit as it touched Alyssa's shirt. She didn't like that book, not one little bit—and that was all there was to it! It gave her the creeps to just have it near her.

They traveled back down the trail they had come up the night before. At the bottom, Blue turned left, taking a rocky path that wound back and forth as it climbed steeply into the Rockroller Mountains.

"Why do they call these the Rockroller Mountains," Brett asked.

"Because most of the Rockrollers live here. A few live in the Impassable Mountains as well."

"What are Rockrollers?" Alyssa asked.

"Small trolls. They're called Rockrollers because they like to roll rocks down onto travelers. They find it immensely amusing. The trolls that live in the Impassable Mountains are generally quite a bit larger and are called Headnockers, because they prefer to sneak up on people and hit them in the back of the head with clubs, although they've also been know to roll rocks as well. They're a great deal more serious about stopping what they consider to be trespassers and therefore more dangerous than Rockrollers."

"Are they going to roll rocks on us?" Brett asked.

The unicorn paused for a moment, thinking this through. "Yesterday," he finally answered. "I would have given you a firm "No", but today I must admit that I'm not sure. Unicorns are the Guardians of Law in Tanzal, and their magic used to be so powerful that Trolls ran from us on sight. Even the Headnockers. Now, I don't know. I guess it depends on how much they know about the destruction of our brotherhood. It really doesn't matter, though, I can outrun most any rock rolled our way, and I am still more than a match for any Troll hatched from a Trollmother's egg. I wouldn't worry too much about it."

"Are you going to run all day?" Alyssa asked, wanting to change the subject. She didn't like talking about people getting knocked in the head by trolls, even if those trolls lived in mountains other than these.

"No. We have a long way to go today, and even a fresh unicorn couldn't run the entire way. After yesterday's race, I shall have to pace myself. But, sometimes, I will have to run or we won't arrive by evening."

Alyssa and Brett got comfortable on the unicorn's back as his step quickened and he picked his way effortlessly up the trail. She noticed that the grass was a little thicker and greener as they climbed, and that there were additional small stands of aspen and birch trees. The scrub oaks and stunted cedars still covered most of the west-facing slopes.

The group spent most of the morning climbing up and down broken hills, sometimes following ridgelines, sometimes down in gulches and stream bottoms, but always heading north. As the sun reached its zenith, they found a shady spot near a stream where the grass was almost waist-high, and Blue stopped to let them off.

"We'll eat lunch here," he said. He promptly proceeded to tear up large mouthfuls of the grass and chew contentedly. After getting a drink out of the stream, which was clear and fresh, Alyssa sat on the bank and tried one of the Norf's biscuits. They had a hard crust, but tasted quite good. She ate three of them. Brett ate four while wading in the stream without his shoes on.

"How much farther do we have?" Alyssa asked.

"Quite a ways. We are almost to the end of the mountains now, only another hour or so, and then I will run again. But it will still be dark before we reach the Starfire River, I'm afraid."

After lunch, the trail became much easier as it flattened out, and Blue picked up the pace. Soon, the hills fell away and they found themselves running on a flat, grass-covered plain that seemed to stretch away forever. Alyssa caught herself dozing off a couple of times through the afternoon.

Brett suddenly nudged her in the ribs. "Look," he said. "Over there." He pointed to their right, and Alyssa spied what looked like a large black dog keeping pace with them. Three more, two of which were white and one grey, loped along behind him. She realized that they were a pack of wolves. She leaned forward on Blue's neck.

"There's something over there," she said.

"Yes, I know," he replied. "We've been in the company of wolves for over an hour. I had to slow down so that they could keep up, but we are much safer now. I was glad when they finally found us."

Alyssa leaned back, confused. Weren't wolves bad? Didn't they always try to eat everything in sight? *Hungry Like the Wolf* was one of her favorite songs. Tanzal was definitely a confusing place, where little old men tried to eat you and the wolves were your guardians! Crazy. She watched as they ran along, keeping perfect pace, but never trying to come any closer.

As the afternoon passed and the sun sank toward the western horizon, she saw purple, snow-tipped mountains rising in the distance. Soon, they arrived at the foot of them and traveled along their base. A small river flowed out of a large canyon and they made their way along its winding banks. The mountains now rose on both sides of them, and off to the right, Alyssa saw a much larger river. She noticed that the wolves had disappeared.

"This is the Terry River," Blue said. "We don't have much further. That's the Starfire that you see over there. It flows from here down to the Azur Sea near Altian."

As they approached where the two rivers met, Alyssa saw a group of small, white ponies grazing along the edge of a large grove of trees. They lifted their heads and neighed at the unicorn as he walked up. Blue neighed back, and the ponies trotted out to greet them. He touched each of their muzzles in turn, nickering softly the entire time. There were seven of them, and Alyssa saw that five had small packs on their backs, and two had riding saddles.

"These are some of the Queen's own ponies," Blue said as they walked toward the trees. "They have consented to carry you and your supplies. They tell me that she has told them about your mission, and they know it will be dangerous, but they consider it a great honor to be asked to help."

At the edge of the grove, Blue knelt down and Alyssa and Brett slid off his back.

"Thank you, Raspal," Blue said, looking at the trees. "I appreciate you're bringing them here."

"Which pony is Raspal?" Alyssa asked, bewildered. Blue was talking to the woods.

"I am Raspal," she heard a small, gravelly voice say from down near her feet, "And I am most definitely *not* a pony."

In amazement, she looked down to see a small red fox curled up on the ground near the base of a large pine. His bushy tail was wrapped around him, covering his feet, and his head rested lightly on it. He was staring up at her in sly amusement.

"As you can see," he continued as he stood and casually stretched his back legs. "I am a fox, and the Queen's chief spy. I am pleased to meet you."

"We're pleased to meet you," Brett replied. Alyssa couldn't think of anything to add. She hadn't talked with a fox before. This was a total trip!

Raspal sauntered out toward the ponies, his tail held high. "You'll have to take the saddles and packs off for the night. I don't have hands so I can't do it. I believe they're full of food, extra clothes, bedding materials and other such stuff that human children need. That must be annoying, having to pack so many things just to stay alive. It makes me glad that I'm a fox."

"How did the packs get put on?" Alyssa asked.

"People did it, of course. I don't put packs *on* either. The ponies were loaded at Tiernan Village."

"And no one came with you to help?"

Raspal shook his head impatiently. "No, they would have only slowed me down. Four legs move faster than two, or haven't you noticed? Anyways, we are at war—they must stay and protect their homes. But I don't mind having to come alone, because a unicorn has thanked me for my efforts! Trust me, children, that doesn't happen everyday. Unicorns don't seem to like us foxes, and we don't know why."

"Ignore him," Blue said. "We have to make allowances for foxes."

"Yes," Raspal replied over his shoulder as he wandered off into the trees toward the river. "Yes we do."

Brett quickly unsaddled the ponies, making sure to memorize how the packs went back on, while Alyssa took inventory of everything. There were extra clothes, sandals, two quilts that buttoned up into sleeping bags, and several pillows. But mostly, there was a large amount of food, including dried meats, cheeses, breads and an assortment of fruits, as well as several water-skins filled with juice. It looked like enough to last two kids a full month. Alyssa was starting to wonder how long the trip to Spellcasting Peak really was.

In the last of the sunlight, Blue and the ponies spread out across the grass to graze, while Brett collected firewood and Alyssa arranged their quilts and pillows. She noticed that Raspal came back after only a minute and curled up near the tree again.

Brett formed a fire pit with a few large stones and carefully stacked some small sticks in the shape of a teepee around a pile of dead pine needles.

"Did you find any matches?" he asked.

"No," Alyssa answered. "I didn't see anything like that. Just food."

"Well, I guess we're not having a fire then. I didn't even think about matches. I have no idea how we'll get it started."

"How do you and dad do it on your hunts?" Alyssa asked. "Didn't you get your Wilderness Survival Merit Badge?"

Brett shook his head. "No," he answered. "I'm taking that next month at Scout Camp. But on the hunts, we always use matches or lighters, along with half a can of gas."

"I know for a fact," Raspal said from the ground. "That they packed a flint and steel. I also had them put in some burning stone. That'll start your fire fast enough."

"So that's what that was!" Alyssa exclaimed, reaching for one of the packs. She pulled out a small leather satchel, which contained a steel bar and two stones. One was hard and black and the other was soft and grey.

"Shave some slivers off the larger stone," Raspal ordered. "And pile them near your tinder. The sparks from your flint and steel will easily light the burning stone."

Brett took the stones from Alyssa and looked carefully at them. "I know what this is," he said. "I'll bet this is magnesium. We did this in science class. This stuff goes up! And I mean fast. It's like gunpowder."

Brett did as Raspal said, and in only a moment, he had a merrily burning campfire. Whatever the rock was made of, it lit on fire the instant that sparks hit the shavings.

Now that his fire was going, Brett pulled his sword out and balanced it in his hand. He pretended to thrust and parry at an invisible foe. The ruins on the blade ran like lightening. Raspal sat up straight and stared in sudden interest.

"I've seen that sword before!" he exclaimed in surprise. "In the painting of Prince Andruson the Young in the Hall of The Liberators. That's the sword of Cabral! Where did you get it?"

"From the Norf's," Blue answered as he stepped into the firelight. "I found it hidden in their cave after I defeated them in battle. I believe they stole it long ago. It has become spoils of war, won honestly, and I have gifted it to Brett. He is its owner, now, by full right. Its magic serves him completely."

"I see," Raspal replied. He seemed impressed for the first time. "It is a beautiful weapon, but if the legends are true, also very strange. They say it fights by itself. You should put it away, Brett, until it is needed. And I would use it with caution."

"I disagree," Blue said. "The boy knows nothing of swords, or swordsmanship. He has had no training at all. When need is upon us, it will be too late to start his lessons. I believe that I should at least teach him the basics, starting tonight."

"*Really*!" Raspal drawled with sarcasm. "The boy holds the Sword of Cabral. It needs no training from a unicorn. It is highly magical. Perhaps *you* will learn something from it!"

Blue snorted in contempt, but didn't answer. He turned his attention to Brett, looking him up and down and appraising his stance.

"Always approach a foe, Brett, with your right foot forward," he said. "Keep your arm slightly bent, and your wrist cocked." Blue bent his head and lifted Brett's wrist with his horn. "And don't hold your sword so far away from you. Keep it closer to your body. Remember, your sword protects you as well as attacks your opponent. Now, let's try a simple parry and thrust."

Blue crossed his horn with the sword. Brett seemed to shiver.

"It makes my arm tingle," he said. "Like electricity's running through it."

The unicorn's horn suddenly spun and thrust toward Brett. But Brett's sword dropped to intercept, catching it easily. The horn and the sword rang out with the sound of steel on steel.

"I didn't do that!" he said in awe. "It did it by itself."

Blue snorted and tried again, this time coming the opposite direction. The sword spun and met him. Blue thrust, but the sword countered. He quickly spun again, then again, and then thrust. Each time the unicorn moved a little quicker, but always the Sword of Cabral met him easily.

Brett's eyes began to gloss over, as though he were falling into a trance.

Suddenly, the sword spun, catching Blue off guard. He barely parried the blow in time. The sword came around again, this time faster. Blue caught it again. Now, the sword spun, then thrust. Blue caught the blows, but snorted in surprise. He took a step backward, but Brett stepped forward, a strange, distant smile on his face. His eyes were completely glazed over.

The sword spun again at Blue, and they began to duel in earnest.

For the first few minutes, Blue and Brett seemed evenly matched, and they both stood their ground. But soon, the sword, its ruins glowing now like gold fire, began to move almost faster than the eye could see, and Blue was forced backwards. His breathing became heavy, and sweat ran down his face. Alyssa saw that he was getting tired.

"That's enough, Brett," she said, but he didn't seem to hear her. He continued to press his advantage. Alyssa didn't know what to do. How were you supposed to stop a sword fight? And what was wrong with Brett?

Suddenly, Brett spun around and the sword dove toward the ground. A small tuft of red fur flew into the air. Raspal had made a run at him. The fox jumped quickly back.

Blue took advantage of the break, and stepped backwards himself several steps. He made sure that he was well out of Brett's reach.

Brett now stood frozen, his blade held high and at the ready. Slowly, his eyes came back into focus, and his sword arm dropped to his side. A look of horror came across his face.

"I'm so sorry," he stammered. "I don't know what happened to me. It was like a dream. I couldn't stop myself. The sword just wanted to attack."

"It's not your fault," Raspal said. He was sitting near his tree again, examining where the sword had cut the fur on his big, bushy tail. Luckily, it hadn't caught the tail itself. "The sword's magic is too strong for you. It took control. Put your blade away, and take it out again only to defend your life."

"Yes," Blue agreed. "Raspal is right. Put it away. And thank you, Raspal, you have saved me from a serious mistake."

The fox suddenly dropped his tail and stared up at Blue with a look of pleasant surprise. "Thanked by a unicorn twice in one day!" he said with a chuckle. "My, my, my! And even more amazing, a unicorn has admitted that a fox was right! Will today's wonders never cease?"

Brett re-sheathed his sword and meekly went and sat next to Alyssa by the fire. She was tempted to say something to him about magic—like "See how scary it can be"—just because of all the razzing he'd given her, but she decided against it. She could see that he felt really bad. He might be the kind to rub it in, but she wasn't. Alyssa prided herself on being the more mature of the two.

With a shock, Alyssa suddenly realized that not ten feet away from them at the edge of the camp stood a huge, jet-black wolf. It had come up without so much as a single whisper of sound, and now stood stone still, its eyes glittering in the firelight. None of the seven ponies—who were now lined up in the trees, sleeping peacefully—or the unicorn seemed to have noticed. Alyssa had no idea what to do! She was frozen with fright. The beast stood over two feet high at the shoulder and looked like it weighed more than her and Brett put together! Its mouth was open slightly, and it fangs looked as long as her fingers.

"Hello, Sturgill," Raspal said casually, glancing up at the wolf. "I see that you've gotten noisy in your old age. I heard you coming at least a hundred yards away. And it sounds like you have at least sixteen of your pack with you."

Three more wolves suddenly appeared in the camp light. Two were white, and one grey, but they weren't near as large as the black one. Alyssa realized that they were the group that had trailed them here. One of the white wolves walked over to the fire, sat on its haunches and lifted a paw and began to lick it. It watched Alyssa and Brett out of the corner of its eye. It made her nervous.

"We weren't trying to be quiet," the black wolf replied. He sounded a little annoyed with the fox. "We heard the sounds of fighting and came as fast as we could. We thought you were in danger."

"The only thing dangerous here," Raspal replied with a chuckle. "Is that unicorn! And that danger is mostly to himself."

"I was giving the boy swordsmanship lessons," Blue replied stiffly. "He needs to be able to defend himself and his sister."

The black wolf arched his eyebrows in surprise. "It sounded like a heated battle to me," he said. "Not anything like lessons."

"Quite a quick learner, wouldn't you say?" Raspal chimed in.

"But we've decided that one lesson will be enough, and we won't be doing *that* anymore. We consider him a Master Swordsman now."

"That's good," Sturgill replied sternly. "We will need him shortly, because Lord Falgerth has sent a pack of Northern Lycants to waylay the Unicorn and his newfound magic. Three of my pack have gone to scout them, and two more are stationed between to relay messages. I estimate that the Lycants will be here by dawn. And they have a troll with them."

"What kind of troll?" Blue asked.

"A Headknocker, and it's a big one, with a big club. Tonas is sure that it has magic. Luckily, Lord Falgerth took his three Black Trolls with him to attack Altian. He is at least five days march away from here, and no concern to us."

"How many Lycants are there?"

"At least thirty, maybe a few more. It's always hard to tell with Lycants. I have fifteen of my pack with me,"—Raspal smiled to himself at this admission, while Sturgill scowled—"as well as the five out scouting. If you were to take out the troll as well as a couple of Lycants, and the boy could handle a couple himself, it should be an even battle. And I do think that we have to consider battle, and choose our own ground. I don't think we can outrun them, not with children and ponies."

"You're right," Blue replied slowly. He stared off into the distance, contemplating the twinkling stars.

"Perhaps," Sturgill ventured. "If you were to go out on your own, it would be best. No one could hope to catch a lone unicorn, and it's you and your magic that Lord Falgerth wishes to stop."

"No," Blue answered. "That may be what Lord Falgerth believes, but it is not true. The Queen couldn't tell you through currier, but I think you should know. I have no special magic. It is in the girl child. Her name is Alyssa. And, Sturgill, from now on, I would like you to be her personal guardian and constant companion. I trust no one else on Tanzal more than you. She needs to be protected at all costs."

The black wolf turned and stared intently at Alyssa. His eyes glittered darkly in the firelight. His attention made her very uncomfortable.

"I will protect her with my life," he answered solemnly. "Which brings us back to the Lycants and their Troll. As I said, they'll be here by early morning, and I don't believe this is a very defensible spot. I don't think we should camp here."

Blue nodded his head in agreement. "What do you suggest?"

"I think we should make for the Starfire Mountains. I know of a spot along the trail where we could make a good defense."

"Raspal, what do you think?" Blue asked, turning to look down at the fox. "That's Gnome country. Your specialty. Do you think that they will bother us?"

"No," Raspal responded immediately. "They are a little braver since the start of the war, I've noticed, but all in all they're still pretty much a bunch of cowards. The sight of ten wolves together would send an entire army of them running for their holes."

"Then it's decided," Blue said. "Let's pack up immediately. Leave the fire going. It should distract them and slow them down. We'll make camp in the Starfire Mountains tonight."

The ponies, without even having to be asked, came and stood next to their packs, and Alyssa helped Brett lift them on. The biggest two took the riding saddles.

While Brett cinched the straps, Alyssa caught the unicorn's eye and pulled him off to one side.

"What are Lycants?" she asked quietly.

"They are dark wolves from the North. Hybrids of evil."

"How can you tell the difference between them and regular wolves?" she asked. "Just so I can stay safe."

Blue's voice was flat and emotionless when he answered.

"Alyssa, when you see a Lycanthropas—a Hybridized Black Wolf—tomorrow morning, you'll understand.

"They are the most evil things you will ever set eyes on."

CHAPTER SIX

Brett in a Hole

Most of that nighttime ride was a tired blur for Alyssa. She'd had to ride all day, and now she was forced to ride into the night. The only good thing was the fact that her pony was completely in charge. It didn't even have a bit or bridle for her to guide it with, like Katie's horse did. Alyssa simply hung onto the saddle horn, while the ponies followed the unicorn in single file.

After a couple of hours, the trail began to climb into dark hills. They hadn't gone up very far when Sturgill—who hadn't left Alyssa's side the entire ride—spoke up.

"This is where I was thinking we should stay, Blue," he said. "There's a small cliff over there where we can camp the ponies and defend them in the morning. They'll be able to come at us from only one direction, and we'll be able to counterattack."

"Fine," Blue replied. "You're the warrior."

The wolf led them into a small hollow and stopped. Brett and Alyssa bailed off their ponies, and walked stiffly around. Alyssa figured that she was about as saddle sore as a person could get. She now realized that riding a pony was much harder on her muscles than riding the unicorn had been. Compared to this, riding Blue had been like riding a magic carpet!

After stretching her legs, Alyssa helped Brett unsaddle and unpack the ponies. They simply dumped the packs into a pile, opening only the one that held their sleeping quilts.

"I'm going to bed," she announced to anyone who cared, and

promptly crawled into her quilt and closed her eyes in order to head off any possible argument. She heard Sturgill come up and lay down next to her. His breathing was deep and raspy. He was a big, black-as-midnight, scary-looking beast, but it made her feel good to have him lying there. He hardly ever spoke, but Alyssa found herself liking him anyways. She peeked through her eyelids over at the wolf—he was on his stomach with his head resting on his paws, but his eyes were actively watching the hills around them. Feeling safe, she closed her eyes and drifted off into sleep.

It seemed like she'd only just fallen asleep when Alyssa felt herself being shook awake. She opened her eyes to find it fully light and Brett standing over her with a steaming cup of brown liquid.

"We let you sleep in," he said. She could hear the excitement in his voice. "Here, I found this in the packs and Raspal showed me how to cook it up. It's just like hot chocolate."

Alyssa sat up and took the cup. She gave it an experimental sip. It was like hot chocolate, only not very strong and it had a woody taste to it. All in all, it was just okay, although it did warm her stomach and woke her right up. She noticed that only Sturgill and the ponies were here in camp.

"Where is everyone?" she asked.

"They've gone to scout the enemy," the wolf relied. He was sitting on his haunches at the edge of camp and watching down the hill. "They're on their way back right now. I can hear them plainly. Even the fox. He isn't as quiet as he thinks he is."

Just then Alyssa spied the unicorn coming up the slope. He had Raspal at his side and seven wolves trailing behind him. She walked over and stood next to Sturgill.

"I thought that you had almost twenty of your pack here?" she said. "I see only seven."

"Remember this Rule of The Wolf, Alyssa. For every one that you see, there are three more wolves that you don't. Lycants are corrupted from years of evil inbreeding. Their senses aren't nearly as keen as ours, so it gives us the advantage of surprise if we stay hidden. Trust me, I have twenty-three wolves all around this camp. Four more joined us in the night. They will attack at my command. Those Lycants don't know what they're walking into."

"But they have a troll," Alyssa objected.

"Yes, but we have a unicorn. I'll take one Unicorn—especially a Blue one and a Captain of Andwar—over a half-dozen trolls any day of the week. This will be a short fight."

Alyssa pondered this as the group approached. She wondered if Sturgill was saying this to reassure her, or if he really believed it. He sounded almost matter-of-fact, like the battle was already over. As she watched, Alyssa noticed that the wolves were disappearing one by one into the undergrowth next to the trail—almost like magic—until once again only the three she'd seen before were left.

"They'll be here in fifteen minutes," Blue said when he arrived. "They're coming straight on with no attempt at hiding. I think they plan to try and overpower us quickly."

"Good," Sturgill said. "That makes our job easier. How many are there exactly?

"Twenty seven," one of the gray wolves answered. "But they're Northern Lycants, from behind the broken shield. They're bigger than the ones we usually fight."

"It doesn't matter," Sturgill replied. "A Lycant's a Lycant. Now let's get ready."

"I noticed that several of your pack walked very close to the Gnome-hole," Raspal said as they made they're way back to the ponies. "You did tell all of them about it, didn't you?"

"Yes, Raspal, I did." Sturgill sounded very annoyed. "They may not be able to see it like you, but they all know exactly where it is."

"Okay, just checking."

"Alyssa," Blue said. "Make sure that you stay close to the ponies. Sturgill will guard you, while Tonas and I attack. Brett, now would be a good time for you to draw your sword and stand next to Sturgill. And whatever happens, protect your sister."

Alyssa moved back until she stood between two of the white

ponies. They didn't seem in the least bit scared, which made her feel better. Behind them, a sheer rock cliff protected their back, while on either side she assumed that wolves were hidden in the sparse trees and bushes. Raspal came and sat next to her. He curled his tail around his front paws.

"I'm not much of a fighter," he confided to Alyssa in a whisper. "I mean, if I could I would, but I think I'd last about two seconds against a Lycant. They're four times my size, and just plain viscous. Finding things out is what I'm good at—and stick to what you can do is what I always say."

"I'm not a fighter either," Alyssa said. "And by the way, what is a Gnome-hole?"

"Oh, it's an entrance to the Gnomes underground Kingdom," Raspal answered. "They connect down to a system of tunnels right beneath us. There's Gnome-holes all over these mountains, but *you* can't see them like I can. They're magically hidden. They blend into the rest of the landscape. It allows the Gnomes to seemingly disappear at will."

"How can you see these holes?"

"I have a special charm on my vision," Raspal answered with a touch of pride. "The Queen cast it on me. One of my main duties as Chief Spy is to keep an eye on the Gnomes. They're not really dangerous, or evil or anything like that, but they're always up to some sort of mischief—sort of like foxes, when you come to think of it. The Queen likes to be kept up on their latest shenanigans. I spend a lot of time under these hills. Now, hush, I hear the troll coming."

With a growing sense of unease, Alyssa watched intently down the hill. Five minutes passed, then ten. Brett began to twirl his sword slowly, back and forth, then around in a circle. Off to her right, the sun rose from behind the hills in a blaze. It was officially daybreak and Alyssa could now hear the sound of heavy footfalls. That must be the troll, she thought. Oh, I hope that Sturgill is right! I hope a unicorn is more than a match for a troll!

Suddenly, the troll appeared around a bend in the trail and came to a stop. It stood stone still, appraising the unicorn and wolves in its path. It was at least ten feet tall and an easy four hundred pounds. The skin on its face and arms was a greasy, brownish red with folds of fat and a huge assortment of warts and lesions. Its massive stomach hung out of what looked like a brown burlap shirt and over burlap pants. It held a wooden club in one hand and a whip in the other. Alyssa thought that it was about the ugliest thing that she had ever seen right up until the Lycants began to come out from behind it.

They were much worse.

Now it wasn't just that they were *ugly*—which they most definitely were—but it was more of a general sense of *wrongness* all about them. To Alyssa, it felt like an aura of evil surrounded them. They were black wolves—or had been many generations ago—but now they were all deformed. Their heads were misshapen and lumpy, and their fangs were twisted and broken, with some rotted completely away. One Lycant was missing an eye, while another looked like it had actually been born with only one. Several were missing legs, and more than one had lost an ear. They growled as they approached, with spit dripping down their curled lips.

Blue reared up and pawed the air, and his blue magic-lights sparkled all around him. His front hooves flashed fire, and his horn glowed. Shaking his head, he neighed loudly. It sounded like a war cry.

When the unicorn came down, the earth rumbled under his feet like an earthquake.

"Nothing but your death awaits you here!" he cried. "Leave while you still have the chance!"

In response, the Lycants charged, followed by the Troll. Blue met them halfway, his flaming hooves flying and his horn darting here and there. His three companion wolves held back and guarded his flanks. At that instant, Sturgill howled long and hard. The hidden wolves suddenly materialized all around the Lycants and attacked. To Alyssa, it looked and sounded like a massive dogfight, with a dueling troll and unicorn in the center of it all.

Suddenly, three Lycants broke free of the melee and charged toward the ponies. And before anyone—not Alyssa, Raspal, or even

Sturgill—could stop him, Brett was striding out to meet them, like a warrior to battle. He spun his sword in a circle as he walked. Its ruins flashed a cold, golden fire.

"Stop him, Sturgill!" Raspal exclaimed. He dashed out a couple of feet and then hesitated, looking back. "He's under the spell of the sword!"

"I cannot," Sturgill replied. "My place is with the girl-child. I dare not leave her."

The three Lycants surrounded Brett and attacked him at once from all sides.

When Brett had dueled with Blue, the Sword of Cabral had moved quickly and expertly, and almost faster than the eye could see. It had easily caught every one of the unicorn's blows. Now, however, with three attackers at the same time, it was much faster. This time, it was nothing but a spinning, silver blur. In an instant, two of the Lycants lay motionless on the ground and the third was running off with its tail tucked firmly between its legs and a large gash on its rear.

Now, Brett waded into the battle in front of him. His sword spun and flashed, up and down, like lightening, leaving Lycants dead all around him. The Sword of Cabral was a cold, driving and merciless killer.

"You're right, Raspal," Sturgill said with a touch of awe in his voice. "He is an expert swordsman. I've never seen anything like him!"

Alyssa's attention was focused on her brother, half scared for him and half in awe of his blade—unlike Sturgill, she knew that he wasn't doing this—but out of the corner of her eye she saw that Blue had torn the whip out of the troll's hands and reduced his club to firewood. And just like Brett, dead Lycants lay all around him. His hooves never seemed to miss anything that came within striking distance.

Alyssa didn't see the unicorn deal the troll a deathblow with his horn, but she did hear the huge man hit the ground with a loud 'thud'. She didn't see this because the moment before the Blue finished off the troll, a large Lycant—almost as big as Sturgill himself—charged at Brett. The beast launched itself into the air three feet before it reached him. The Sword of Cabral came around, pointing upward, and the Lycant impaled himself on the blade up to its hilt.

But the Lycant's momentum knocked Brett over and the two rolled backward on the ground.

And then they disappeared.

Alyssa gave out a sudden gasp of fright. One moment, her brother had been there, and the next instant, he was gone. No flashes of light, no puffs of smoke, no fireworks. He and the dead Lycant on his sword had simply vanished into thin air.

"Oh, no!" Raspal moaned. "He's fallen. He's down the Gnome hole."

"Just what we didn't need," Sturgill said.

Now that the troll was dead, Blue turned his attention to the remaining Lycants. There were only eight left alive, and when they saw that their pack leader had vanished, their troll was dead, and a unicorn was heading toward them, they turned tail and ran.

Sturgill's pack chased them down the trail, howling victoriously as they followed.

Blue surveyed the battle scene to make sure no enemies were left, then turned and trotted over to the group by the ponies.

"Where's Brett?" he asked, looking around. "I saw him fighting. He did very well. He isn't hurt, is he?"

"We don't know if he's hurt or not," Sturgill answered. "He fell into the Gnome hole. A Lycant fell with him, but I'm sure it's dead."

"Alyssa, I'm going to need supplies," Raspal stated suddenly. "There's a small knapsack in one of the horse's bags. Fill it with three days worth of food for Brett, and a bag of that deer-jerky for me. I don't imagine anyone's got an egg or two, do they?"

Looking glum, Blue shook his head no. Sturgill did the same.

"You didn't see any eggs when you went through the packs did you, Alyssa?" Raspal asked.

"No, none. What do you want eggs for?"

Raspal sighed. "The Gnomes," he said. "I can't believe that I didn't bring my egg pack, but, then again, I didn't know I was going down into the Gnome Kingdom. Oh, well, it can't be helped now. I'll just have to do without it."

Alyssa did as she was asked, and rummaged through the horse bags until she found the small knapsack. She loaded it with bread, cheese and jerky while she watched Blue, Sturgill and Raspal walk down the trail to where Brett had disappeared. They talked too quietly for her to hear as they stared at the ground. When it was full, she took the bag down to them. She did her best to not look directly at the dead Lycants or the Troll.

"Do you think that Brett's okay?" she asked when she arrived.

"He's alive," Blue said. "I used magic to feel down there. But I can't tell if he's hurt or not—or how badly."

"Can we just drop a rope to him? Or just wait for him to climb out? He can climb cliffs and rocks. We both can. We go with our dad almost every weekend."

"No," Raspal answered. "This Gnome-hole is over a hundred feet deep. We don't have nearly enough rope. Also, it's a magical One-Way hole. Even if he can climb, the spell on this hole wouldn't let him."

"A hundred feet!" Alyssa gasped. "Straight down? If he's not dead, then he's probably broke every bone in his body."

"No," Raspal said, shaking his head. "It's only straight down for about the first ten feet. After that, it starts to gradually slope until it's almost flat. I've rolled down them a hundred times. I'm sure he's fine. Now, I've got to get going. He's probably set off the alarm and the Gnomes could come by at any time and find him. Hand me that bag, please, Alyssa."

She sat the small knapsack on the ground in front of him and Raspal rummaged through it. Looking satisfied, he quickly retied the drawstrings with his paws and teeth. Alyssa was amazed at how deftly he was able to do this. That was one tricky fox! He then picked it up with his mouth and turned and dropped it on the ground behind him.

Only it didn't hit the ground.

Instead, it simply disappeared. Alyssa gave a little gasp of surprise, and Raspal chuckled at her.

"Okay," he said. "I have to go. Remember, if we're not out of the Treestone Mine Entrance by noon tomorrow, come in and get us. We'll either be out, or we'll need to be rescued. I'll see you there."

At that, Raspal turned, took two steps forward, and vanished into thin air.

Alyssa stared intently at the ground where he had gone, but could see nothing but more dirt, grass and rocks. It was so bizarre. Carefully, she knelt down and reached forward to touch it.

"Don't get too close," Sturgill warned. He took a step toward her. "We don't need you down there too."

"I won't," she answered. "This is as far as I'll go. I just want to touch it."

"But there's nothing to touch," Blue said.

Alyssa didn't answer that. The unicorn didn't understand. He'd been born and raised with magic. This was as strange to her as a television set would be to him. Her hand was now where her eyes told her that the earth should be, but she felt nothing but air. It was the strangest sensation that she'd ever had—almost as strange as feeling the invisible box that the Fourth Book of Magic had been hidden in. She pushed down a little more and her hand disappeared into the illusion of ground up to her wrist. With a jerk, she pulled it back out. She didn't like that at all.

"How do they do it?" she asked.

"Magic," Blue answered. His tone said that he was a little confused by the question. "It's not even very good magic. Anyone with talent can see right through it. Gnomes really aren't very magical. They're just good at digging in the earth."

Alyssa stood and looked over her shoulder at the ponies. They were calmly munching on grass as if nothing had happened—as if battles and dead Lycants were an everyday occurrence.

"I guess we should be going," she finally said because nobody seemed to be moving.

"No," Blue replied. "We're giving Raspal a few minutes. If Brett is badly injured, he's going to come back up—he's the only creature who can do that on a One-Way tunnel—and Sturgill is going to send down some wolves to carry him to the Treestone Mine Entrance."

"Shouldn't some wolves go and help anyway?" Alyssa asked.

"That's hard to say," Sturgill said. "We talked about it while you packed the food. I think a wolf escort would help, but Blue and Raspal believe that they're better off trying to sneak Brett out. More animals and more of a chance at getting caught—I guess."

"Think about it, Sturgill," Blue said. "How much more of a defense would a couple of wolves be? You seen that boy with his sword. He killed as many Lycants as your entire pack, and in half the time! The only way he could be any safer is if he had a dozen eggs with him for throwing!"

"What is it with the eggs?" Alyssa asked. "I don't get it."

"Gnomes are deathly afraid of eggs," Sturgill answered. "You see, Gnomes never get old, and the only way they die is if they're killed by accident or in battle—or, if they're touched by any part of an egg, inside or out. If an egg touches them, they start to age just like everyone else and eventually they will die of old age. They consider it the most horrible thing that could ever happen. They flee from the very sight of an egg."

"That's why you hardly ever see Gnomes aboveground," Blue added. "The thought of walking through the woods and accidentally stumbling into a bird's nest full of eggs terrifies them."

"I see," Alyssa said. "I guess it's too bad that we didn't have any of them. How long are we supposed to wait here?"

"A few more minutes," Blue said. "Just to be safe. If you want, you can be putting the packs on the ponies."

Alyssa nodded and walked back to the camp. She had to do something. She couldn't just stand around. Without being asked, the ponies stopped chewing grass and lined up next to their packs. She decided that even though they might not be able to talk, they fully understood what was being said around them. The first pony she saddled was the one that she rode, and the entire time she worked, it kept nickering and nudging her in the side.

"What?" she finally asked. "Am I doing something wrong?"

The little horse whinnied and stepped forward. It walked back to the end of the line, bent its head and pushed at one of the packs.

"Is there something in there I need to use?"

The pony bobbed its head up and down, as if to say 'yes', and stamped the ground with its front hoof. Alyssa kneeled and opened the pack. It was the one filled with the assorted fruit. She saw that over half of the fruits inside were red apples. She pulled a large, dark one out and held it up.

"You want an apple, don't you?" she said with a laugh. The pony stamped the ground again. "But if I give you an apple, then I have to give everybody one!"

The other ponies all whinnied their agreement. She looked over at them and saw that they were watching her intently. How could she say no? They were all working so hard—not to mention risking their lives—to help her and Brett get back home.

"Oh, okay," she relented. "But only half an apple each. We have to save some of them for later."

The ponies nickered happily, and then began to stomp impatiently while Alyssa fished around in another pack for a knife. When she found one, she picked out four of the largest apples and cut them in half. Then she walked down the line, giving each one of the seven ponies their portion. There was a half left over, and Alyssa ate this herself. It was the sweetest apple she had ever tasted, and she was tempted to get herself a second one but decided that it wouldn't be polite to eat another in front of the ponies. She would sneak one out later.

By the time Alyssa had finished loading the ponies, Blue and Sturgill came over and appeared ready to go.

"I see that the ponies have gotten a treat," Blue remarked, looking up and down the line. "Was it their idea, or yours, Alyssa?"

"Mostly theirs," she answered. "But I figured a couple of apples wouldn't hurt them. I wasn't wrong, was I?

"No, of course not," Blue replied. "But for future reference, Alyssa, be aware that Unicorns like apples as much as horses— especially the ones from the hills above Tiernan Village."

"Do you want me to get you one, too?" Alyssa asked.

Blue laughed out loud. "No," he replied. "I'll get myself one later. Now, we should be going."

Alyssa pulled herself up into her saddle and shifted around until she was comfortable. Her muscles were still sore from the day before and she wasn't looking forward to the long ride ahead. Without another word, the unicorn headed down the trail, making his way between the dead Lycants. Alyssa's pony followed right behind him, and the others came in single file. Sturgill trailed along next to her.

"What's going to happen to those…things?" she asked the wolf, nodding at the Lycants.

"Don't worry," he said. "My pack will come back and take care of them. They are diseased and best buried."

Just then, a chorus of wolves howled in the distance. Sturgill stopped and listened, and then howled himself in return. It lasted a good minute or more, and even though he stopped and trotted back up to Alyssa's side, his pack in the distance continued on.

"What is that about?" she asked.

"They tell me that the rest of the Lycants are dead, and that three of our pack are also gone. They howl their names and mourn their loss, as do I, but I must stay with you as well, so I will do my mourning in silence. They also howl to release their pain. It is the way of the wolf."

Alyssa pondered this in silence as they made their way forward. For over an hour, the group traveled due west, which was basically a left hand turn from the direction that they had been going. They climbed into steep, pine-covered hills where the trail was rocky and twisting. But the ponies didn't seem put out at all. They were surefooted and easily kept up with the fast moving unicorn.

As they went, Alyssa wondered what was happening with Brett. It felt strange not to have him here. She hoped that he was okay—that he hadn't hurt himself in the fall. Despite all his faults and smart-aleck remarks, she did love her little brother.

At a switchback in the trail, Blue stopped and took a breather. Alyssa figured that it was more for the ponies' sake than his own. He didn't look like he was winded at all.

"How much farther is this mine entrance?" Alyssa asked.

"We won't be there until tomorrow in the morning, at the earliest," Blue answered. "And it's more likely to be early afternoon."

"Will Brett and Raspal make it as quick?"

"Oh, easily," Blue answered. "They're going in a direct line under the mountains, whereas we're going around and about and over the top of them. Our path is easily three times as long as theirs. They'll have to hide inside and wait for us before they try to escape tomorrow. I'm sure that they'll need our help. That entrance is always guarded."

Alyssa thought about this for a minute. She wasn't exactly sure what the plan was here, but she always felt better if there was one. Maybe Raspal had come up with one down in the caves, but that didn't really reassure her much. She liked the fox, but he didn't inspire a great deal of confidence in her. He didn't seem much more mature than Brett, and was just as big a smart aleck.

"But what if the Gnomes catch them and won't let them out?" she asked.

"Then they'll face something even more terrifying than eggs," the unicorn answered grimly.

"The Gnomes will meet an angry Blue Unicorn!"

CHAPTER SEVEN

Gnomes, Gnomes, Everywhere

Now, like Alyssa, you're probably wondering what happened to Brett, and if he was okay.

Well, when Brett had first drawn the Sword of Cabral, just before the Troll appeared, it had hummed slightly in his hands, sending vibrations of excitement running through him. He had started to slowly spin it—waiting—and the sword's spell had begun to work upon him. He had come to realize that when the ruins were flashing, its magic was working. He could feel himself falling under its influence, slipping slowly into a trancelike state. But even if Brett could have stopped it—which he didn't think he could—he really didn't want to. It made him feel good. It made him feel strong. It made him feel like he could conquer anything!

When the troll came around the corner, Brett felt another, stronger thrill. It marched up and down inside him. It was time for battle! He spun the Sword of Cabral even faster.

But when the Lycants appeared, the sword sent out waves of anger. It hated Lycants. Their feud went back a thousand years. The very sight of them drove it crazy.

It was only because Brett wasn't fully under the spell—he wasn't actually in the act of fighting and was able to exert a small amount of restraint—that he didn't attack at the very first sight of the Lycants.

When the three Lycants charged toward them, his small amount of resistance gave way in a rush.

What happened next was like a waking dream for Brett. The

sword was in complete control, and it drug him into battle and attacked without mercy.

It was only when the sword was torn from his hands as he and the dead Lycant tumbled down the Gnome-hole, that the spell was broken.

Luckily for Brett, Raspal had been right, and this Gnome-hole gradually sloped as it dropped, and he came to a gentle stop down where the ground was almost level.

Picking himself up, Brett dusted off the dirt and gravel on his shirt and pants and looked around. The opening far above him faintly lit the hole he'd fallen in, and as his eyes adjusted to the dark, Brett saw that he was in fact inside a tunnel of some sort, and not a cave. It looked like the walls around him had been hewn out of solid rock with picks and shovels. He ran his hands along the wall. The gray stone was cold and hard and uneven.

Brett now saw that the dead Lycant had rolled even farther than him, and he walked down and pulled his sword free of its body. He cleaned his blade on the evil wolf's back, but didn't sheath it. It was no longer tingling, but Brett didn't want to chance putting it away down here. Who knew what could come along? He had to be ready for anything.

Turning around, Brett decided that he might as well climb back up. He hadn't gotten a real good look at the sides of the tunnel, but he couldn't imagine there not being any good holds—or it being any harder than the *Mall Walls* he'd climbed when he was younger. At the very least he could yell to Alyssa and the Unicorn for help if the climb was too smooth. Maybe they could drop a rope to him. He took several steps up the slope, and to his amazement found that he wasn't moving! He tried again, but still didn't go anywhere.

Brett looked down at his feet the next time he tried and saw that they were simply sliding over the top of the dirt without moving so much as a single grain of it. He almost laughed out loud. He was doing the Michael Jackson Moonwalk and wasn't even trying!

Okay, he decided, this was a bunch of garbage. He wasn't going to be stuck here, like some idiot fly caught in a magic spider web.

Brett turned and walked down the slope and found that he could move that direction with no problem. He then turned around and again tried to walk up. It didn't work. He couldn't even make it back to where he'd been! This was apparently a one-way tunnel, and he didn't have the magic needed to get out.

At that moment, a small brown knapsack came rolling down the hill and landed at Brett's feet. He picked it up and opened it. It was full of food.

Great he thought. *Sorry we can't get you out, Brett! But here's some food so you won't starve. We'll be back when we finish our mission. Good luck!*

He shook his head. No way. Alyssa would never do that to him. He knew his sister. But then again, she wasn't in charge up there. There wasn't even a note inside, telling him what to do. What the heck was going on here?

"Well, I'm glad to see that you're all in one piece," a voice said from the ground. Brett jumped halfway to the ceiling. He squinted into the gloom near the wall and spotted Raspal slinking toward him.

"Don't do that," he complained. "You about scared me to death!"

Raspal chuckled. "Always be on your toes, my boy. You never know what's sneaking up on you. Now, did you try and climb back up?"

"Yes!" Brett exclaimed. "But I can't! My feet just slide over the top of the earth."

"Not so loud, Brett," Raspal said in a whisper for emphasis. "From now on, think silence and sneakiness. We're in Gnome country, and they don't take kindly to intruders. You can't go back because it's a magic sand trap, and by trying to leave, you've set off their alarm. I'm sure that they're on their way right now."

"I didn't know that," Brett said defensively.

"Of course you didn't," Raspal answered. "There's no way you could have. But nevertheless, we've got to move fast. I know of a side tunnel that we can hide in, but we'll have to reach it before they cut us off. You'll have to run."

"I can't run down a strange tunnel in pitch blackness," Brett said in a matter-of-fact type of whisper. "Remember, I'm not a fox."

"This is true," Raspal answered. "Which is too bad for you." He then muttered something under his breath and suddenly a floating ball of light appeared. It bobbed in the air about a foot above Brett's head and gave off a brownish-red glow, which was the exact same color as Raspal's fur.

Brett gave a little gasp. "How did you do that?"

"Magic," Raspal answered smugly. "I have a natural, inborn magic, which for a fox is extremely rare. The Queen has taught me quite a few spells. Now you can run. Let's go!"

And with that, the fox turned and darted down the tunnel. Brett sheathed his sword and ran after him, while the orb of light followed along directly above him, lighting his way perfectly.

The slope of the tunnel was fairly steep at first, and it seemed to Brett that they must be running down into the very center of the earth. But after a while, it started to level out as it veered to the left. He now thought that he could hear the distant sound of an underground river, roaring along somewhere in the blackness far below them.

As they ran past a dark side tunnel that dove steeply down, Brett felt a rush of cold, damp air hit his face. He could hear the river now distinctly. It sounded as if it was huge, and Brett was glad that they weren't going that way.

After the opening, the tunnel began to gradually climb, and the running became harder, but it wasn't too bad. Brett had done much worse in football and baseball practice.

Suddenly, Raspal came to a stop. "Shhh," he said as he cocked one ear toward the front of them. Brett stood perfectly still for a full minute, watching the ball of light bob up and down and trying his best not to breath too loudly.

"We've lost that race," Raspal finally said. "Eight or nine Gnomes are coming this way."

"What'll we do?"

The fox sat and thought for a moment. "It's a dead end behind us, even down to the underground Starfire River. I really don't see that we have much of a choice. Draw your sword, Brett. We'll have to try and reason with them."

Brett pulled out the Sword of Cabral and saw that its ruins were faintly flashing. It hummed slightly in his hands. But the magic felt different this time. It didn't seem like it wanted to take Brett over, and it wasn't in the least bit fierce or angry. The sword felt as if it only wanted to protect him, not attack. Brett marveled at this—it seemed to have moods like a person.

"I'll do the talking," Raspal said stepping back to Brett's side. "And you do the fighting. One way or another, the only way we can go is forward."

After a few minutes, Brett could make out a faint white, light reflected on the distant tunnel walls. It bobbed up and down as it drew closer. Now, he could hear distant voices.

"I do hope that's its a deer," a high squeaky voice was saying. "We haven't had a good venison steak in forever!"

There was a chorus of general agreement, and Brett decided that they must feel fairy safe to talk so loudly. It was after all their kingdom. A minute later, the group rounded a curve in the tunnel and came face to face with Brett and the fox. All nine of them came to a sudden stop and stared in amazement. It was the first time Brett had ever laid eyes on a Gnome, and he was surprised at how much they looked like the Norfs. They were small men—even smaller than him—and their skin was pale white and gnarled. They had pointed little heads with thick, spiked hair, and tiny, wiry hands. Each wore a white tunic, which was held on by a sword belt, and several wore gold necklaces with small, greenish stones on them. Two of the men were carrying lanterns, which swung on their handles and threw shadows back and forth.

One of the Gnomes—the one in charge Brett decided—pulled out his sword and stepped forward.

"You are trespassing in Gnome country!" he proclaimed loudly. "You are under arrest. Put down your weapons!"

"We humbly beg your pardon, Maltheus," Raspal answered. "But we didn't mean to come here. We fell into a hidden hole and couldn't leave. We mean no harm and cordially request a friendly escort to the outside of the Gnome's Kingdom."

The little man jumped at the mention of his name, and now squinted suspiciously down at Raspal. "How do you know who I am?" he asked. "I don't recall ever seeing you before. And I don't consort with foxes!"

"I know of you from your heart-shaped Tanzalite gemstone," Raspal replied in a humble voice. "There are very few cut like it, and no other of that size."

"I see," the Gnome replied. He seemed lost in thought for a moment, while he fingered the small, green stone that hung on his gold necklace. It was surrounded by several smaller white and green gemstones.

"Nevertheless," he finally continued, "you must put down your weapons and come with us. I will take you before the king. He will decide your fate."

"We will gladly go with you to the King," Raspal answered. "But I'm afraid that we cannot surrender our weapons. We must be able to defend ourselves."

"The penalty for trespassing and resisting arrest is death," the little man said ominously. "I will give you one last chance. Put down your sword or we will take it from you."

Raspal took a step backward in order to stay out of Brett's way.

"I think that you'll need more than just the nine of you," he said with a chuckle.

"We will see," the leader said grimly, brandishing his short sword. He took a step forward as the other eight Gnomes drew their blades as well. Maltheus made a quick jab at Brett, but the Sword of Cabral came around in a sudden sweep, catching it easily. The Sword then gave a quick flick and the Gnome leader's weapon went flying down the tunnel behind Brett. He heard it clatter against the rock wall and then hit the ground.

Maltheus gasped, as though this kind of thing had never happened to him before, and fell back. Three more Gnomes took his place. They attacked fiercely, but one by one their swords were ripped from their grips and flung down the tunnel.

This continued until only two Gnomes still had blades. By then all nine were stunned at Brett's apparently incredible skill and retreated several steps. Not a single Gnome had received so much as scratch from the fighting. The Sword didn't seem to want to hurt the little men, only stop their attack.

"Look," one of the Gnomes suddenly exclaimed. "He holds the Sword of Cabral. And the legends are true! Look at the size of that Stone! I have never beheld its like."

All the Gnomes gave gasps of sudden wonder. "The great Stone of Sword," several muttered. "It has finally come back to us," another exclaimed.

"We must tell the King," Maltheus said, and all nine men turned as one and disappeared into the darkness. They left behind their two lanterns.

"This is not good," Raspal said. "This is not good at all. Come on."

"What's not good?"

"I'll tell you later. "We have to move fast. Don't ask questions. Just follow me."

The fox scampered off at quick run, and Brett followed, his brown light bobbing along above him and keeping perfect pace.

For quite a ways, the tunnel was pretty much the same as it had been, wide and flat and slightly uphill. But before long, it started to close in and get steeper. Large stones now lay here and there, and Brett had to watch closely so that he didn't stumble on them. He pretended that he was dodging linebackers on the football field.

Suddenly, Raspal took a quick right turn toward the tunnel wall and vanished into the solid rock. Brett stopped and stared in amazement. There was no sign whatsoever of the fox; he was all alone now. More magic, no doubt, he thought to himself. But it would be nice if the fox would let him know about it beforehand—and an explanation about what he was supposed to do would be kind of handy as well.

Just then, Raspal's head poked out of the solid wall. There was no sign at all of his body. It looked for all the world to Brett like a stuffed fox's head hanging on a cave wall. Only this fox's head was laughing at him.

"I'm sorry," Raspal's head chuckled. "I forgot that you can't see the hidden Gnome holes. Sheath your sword now—you won't need it for a while—and get down on your hands and knees and crawl into the tunnel wall right where I'm at. Trust me, there's a hole here."

Brett did as he was told and to his amazement discovered that he could slip easily into what looked like solid rock. Once in, he found that he was now in a much smaller tunnel, which was barely big enough for him to fit on his hands and knees. Glancing over his shoulder, he could clearly see the hole that he'd come through and the main tunnel beyond. This magic was a lot like one of those famous FBI two-way mirrors.

"*Latius Atimues!*" Raspal said in a firm voice, and small, brownish-red magic lights sparkled for a moment all around the two of them.

"What's that about?" Brett asked.

"I've reversed the Gnome's magic cover on them," Raspal answered with a laugh. "I love doing that. It makes it so that they can't see their own hole. Whenever I catch them on the surface, I always change the closest Gnome-holes. Sometimes they're lost for days. Now, they'll have no idea which way we went. Come on. And do try to keep up!"

And off the fox went, gleefully scampering as if this was the most fun that he'd had in a long time.

For the next couple of hours, Brett followed Raspal's tail. At first, they crawled through a series of closed in and steep tunnels, which wound first right and then left, and sometimes went up, but mostly down. The two often crossed main tunnels—always stopping and listening for a few minutes before they did—but mostly they kept to the smaller side caves. They also passed through several more of the hidden tunnel *'covers'*, some of which Raspal magically reversed and some of which he didn't. Brett didn't have a clue as to why he altered some and not others—and there wasn't really any time to ask.

After a while, the tunnel walls they passed began to change. It gradually became less rocky and hard and began to have deposits of soil and sand. Now, Raspal slowed his fast pace, and he often stopped and listened intently. His pointy ears continually flicked around, this way and that, so that he could hear in all directions.

When they had passed through another *'cover'* that led into a small, low cavern, Raspal stopped and sat down.

"You might as well relax, Brett," he said. "We've come as far as we can go for now. We'll have to wait here until tomorrow morning."

"They won't find us here?"

"No. I changed the magic cover to this little cavern several years ago, and they've never discovered it. I've also put a soundproofing charm on it. We're completely sealed in. This is where I sleep when I'm down here on extended spying trips."

Brett gratefully sat down. The floor of the grotto was made of soft dirt. He took off his backpack and fished out the water bottle. After a run like that, he needed a drink. He also found a small bowl and poured some for the fox as well.

"Why do we have to wait until morning?" Brett asked as he rooted around in his pack for something to eat.

"Because we came straight through this mountain range," Raspal answered. "Blue and your sister will have to take a trail that goes both around and over. It's a lot longer. And I don't dare try to escape from here until they're outside the mine entrance, you know, for backup. Hey, I believe your sister packed some deer jerky for me. Pass some over, would you?"

Brett obliged the fox and handed him some. "So now we've got a break," he said between bites of a biscuit that he'd pulled out for himself. "Maybe you can tell me why those Gnomes were so surprised at my sword. They were in awe of it—like it was almost a religious item, or something."

Raspal chuckled to himself. "Well, for them, in a sense, it is. It's a long story—legend, actually—but I guess we've got nothing better to do, do we? Let's see, where do I start?

"First you need to know about Tanzalite. That's the gemstone that the Gnomes mine down here, and it's the most prized material in all of Tanzal. It's also the hardest stone there is."

"On Earth we have diamonds," Brett interrupted. "They're the hardest stone of all."

"We have diamonds as well," Raspal answered with a smile. "But on Tanzal, they're the second hardest stone. Tanzalite can scratch a diamond, but a diamond can't scratch Tanzalite. That makes Tanzalite the harder of the two.

"But that's not why it's so valuable. You see, cut Tanzalite holds magic. Necklaces and rings adorned with spellbound stones can hold great power—and sometimes it's ancient magic that was put into it ages ago. Magic is always changing—a charm that worked one day one way, may not work exactly the same the next—but once it is cast into Tanzalite, it stays forever the same.

"The problem is, small stones can only hold small spells, and the larger stones are extremely rare. Anything over the size of a pebble is considered huge, by aboveground standards, and can hold immense power. No one knows for sure how many good-sized gems the Gnomes have stashed away, but only a few every year are traded by them.

"However, the Gnomes can't cast strong magic—they're really not very magical, and I believe it has something to do with their immortality—and so if they want power put into their stones, they have to trade with magician's and Elves on Tanzal's surface.

"That's where the Sword of Cabral came from. Draw it, Brett, and let me show you something."

Brett did as he was asked and pulled his sword free.

"I guess you've noticed that gem on your sword, haven't you?"

"Of course," Brett answered. He once again looked at the dark green gemstone embedded at the end of the steel handle. It was easily the size of a golf ball, and cut with a thousand facets. Even in the dim, brown light of Raspal's magic orb, it glinted like an incredible, green diamond.

"That is the largest piece of Tanzalite ever found," Raspal said solemnly. "It is easily three—and more likely four—times larger than the next known stone. It isn't just big, Brett, it's massive.

"And it's full of Elvish magic. You see, legend has it that the Gnomes of old traded the Elves a large bag of uncut Tanzalite stones for the creation of the Sword of Cabral. The price was high because the forging of the sword, the cutting of the stone, and the casting of the spells, took many years, and a great deal of elvish magic went into it.

"But the Gnome King, Cabral, never received his sword when it was finished. A convoy of Gnomes made the final payment on it, took possession, and headed home, but they never made it back to the Starfire Mountains. Instead, they were waylaid by an army of Harriden Warriors—aided by their sighted witches—out of the desolate north.

"Gnomish history blames the Elves for the loss. They claim that the Elves should have delivered the sword safely to the Gnome Kingdom. But the Elves blame the Gnomes for sending too small a contingent to protect it properly—and, anyways, they never asked that it be delivered directly to their Kingdom. Either way, it was gone.

"A few years after that, Gamadrin The Conqueror sacked Sarasilin, the capital of Harriden, and he took the sword back with him to the Southern Reaches. Of course, the Gnomes demanded its return, but it had become spoils of war—fairly won—and so of course was kept by the Southern Kings. It became a weapon for the Crown Prince of the Royal family, to keep him safe from assassination and attack by Lycants and other evil things.

"But a little over a hundred years ago, the sword was stolen from the Royals, and no one had heard anything about it until now. It was always assumed that the Gnomes had stolen it—even though they denied it adamantly—and were keeping it hidden. Now, I guess, we know the truth. The Norf's either took it, or, more likely, had it stolen for them.

"And now you have it, my boy," Raspal finished. "Courtesy of a Blue Unicorn."

"Wow," Brett breathed in awe. He slowly turned his sword and stared at it with new wonder. "This was a heckuva a nice thing for

Blue to let me have—even if it is only for a short time. I had no idea it was this valuable."

"Yes," Raspal admitted. "It was very nice of him, wasn't it? But then again, as far as Unicorns go, he's always been the best sort. I really should be nicer to him. Most Unicorns are arrogant Asses—no pun intended—full of strong magic and power and thoroughly convinced that they're better than everyone else. But Blue's always been a quiet sort of unicorn, reserved really, and he's actually quite considerate of other people—even foxes. Of course, it's because he's blue. It's quite a weight, I suppose, to be a young Blue Unicorn and always wondering what your Quest will be, and if you'll measure up to the Great Task ahead of you."

Brett looked up from his sword at this. "Quest?" he asked. "What Quest? What do you mean?"

"Blue never told you, did he?" Raspal chuckled to himself. "Of course he didn't. He's embarrassed by it. Well, then, I'll tell you for him.

"Unicorns aren't normally blue. They're brown, black, sorrel—generally the same colors as horses—but once in about every fifty generations, a pure white unicorn colt is born, who, when he comes to maturity at the age of five, will grow a horn of pure silver. He is known as the First Silver Sentinel, and exactly one year to the day after his birth, a second pure white unicorn is born; this is the Second Silver Sentinel. On the second birthday, the Chief of Andwar—that's the leader of the unicorns—and his mare will foal a third white unicorn. He is the Third Silver Sentinel, and he will grow to be the fastest, tallest and strongest of any unicorn ever born. He will also be the most magically powerful of any unicorn—except for one other.

"Five years after the Third Silver Sentinel is born, The Chief of Andwar and his mare will foal again, only this time, they will have a Blue Unicorn for a colt. He isn't large and strong, like his Silver Sentinels, but his natural, inborn magic is greater than that of any other woodland creature's and often rivals the abilities of even the greatest of magicians. This is a rare and wondrous event, and a time of celebration for the Unicorns. But it's also a time of fear. Because, you see, every Blue Unicorn and his Silver Sentinels at some time in their adult lives will be faced with a Great Magical Task—The Unicorn's Quest. It's what they were foaled for, and it usually comes at a time of war and strife. The foaling of the Three Silver Sentinels and then the Blue Unicorn often means that troubled times are ahead—and a hero is needed in Tanzal.

"And as you can see, the legends are true. We have the Three Silver Sentinels, The Blue Unicorn, war—and now we have a Great Quest!"

"You mean helping me and my sister get back home is his Great Quest?" Brett asked in wonder.

Raspal laughed out loud at this. He seemed to think that everything anyone else said or did was funny—and Brett had no idea why.

"No. Finding you and your sister and defeating the Norfs in magical battle was just the beginning of his labors. If he protects and helps your sister use The Ancient One's Magic to rebuild the Great Northern Shield, then this, I think, will be known as his Great Quest.

"But remember, Brett, Blue Unicorns don't always complete their Quests. A great many over the years have failed. Having a Blue Unicorn on our side is no guarantee that any of us will make it through."

"I see," Brett said. "Well, I still hope he helps us get back home."

"So do I. But first we have to escape the Gnomes, and my internal clock tells me that it's almost evening. We need to get some sleep. We may have to fight our way out of here tomorrow."

Brett agreed and tried to get comfortable lying on the dirt. He used the knapsack of food for a makeshift pillow, and Raspal muttered something under his breath, and his brown light went out.

"You know," Brett said just before he fell asleep, "I don't think that my sword wanted to fight the Gnomes today. It seemed to do as little as possible."

"I noticed that," Raspal answered. "And I was a little surprised. But we must remember, Brett, the Gnomes never really owned it, and it is bound to you by Gift, and governed by Old Magic. I have a feeling that your sword only attacks when absolutely necessary. But, trust me, it *will* do everything in it's power to keep you safe."

As he drifted off, Brett thought that maybe Raspal didn't know as much as he thought he did. The Sword of Cabral had literally drug him into battle against the Lycants, and unless his dreamlike state caused false memories, the feeling he'd gotten from the sword was one of joy at their destruction. It hated Lycants—totally and completely.

But it didn't hate the Gnomes. Not at all.

When Brett woke again, he wasn't sure if it was morning or not. The cavern was still pitch black, and he could hear the light breathing of Raspal at his side, but nothing else. He tried to go back to sleep, but couldn't. He wasn't tired at all. It must be morning, he thought. It *felt* like morning anyway.

"Raspal," he whispered. "Are you awake?"

"No need to whisper," the fox replied. "And yes, I'm awake." He muttered something to himself, and his magic orb reappeared in the air above Brett. "I was waiting for you to awaken. Let's eat breakfast. We need to be going."

Brett fished out some more jerky and biscuits, and the two ate in silence. When they were finished, Brett reloaded the knapsack and slung it over his shoulder.

"Follow me closely," Raspal whispered as they slipped through the magical entrance. "And don't speak unless I ask a question. Now, come on."

They followed the small tunnel for only a short distance before they came to a main thoroughfare. This one was wider and taller than any they'd come to yet. It was at least fifteen feet wide and ten feet tall, and it's floor was made of closely-fitted flat stones. It had a gentle rise to it, and the air felt fresher and moved slightly. Raspal stopped and listened, and then without a word, made his way up it. He held to the right-hand tunnel wall, stopping every once in a while to listen intently.

"I hear someone coming," he finally whispered at one of his stops. "I was afraid of this. We'll have to go around. We can skirt the amphitheater and get to the entrance from the southern side. We actually came a lot further than I thought we would."

The fox quickly found a side cave on the left, and Brett followed him into it. Before long, it narrowed down to the point where Brett had to hunch over in order to walk. Suddenly, it opened up into a good-sized cavern with three large tunnels leading off from it. Raspal listened intently at each of the three entrances.

"This is not good," he finally said. "I can hear Gnomes behind us now. I think that they've caught our scent or something. And I can hear them moving in both the North and the South corridors. There's several large parties both directions. The only place that's quiet is the Amphitheater itself, but we can't use my light in there—magic use would set off alarms. We'll have to go through it in the dark, and we'll have to go fast."

Brett shook his head. "You know I can't see in the dark. It won't work. I'll stumble around and walk into the walls."

"I know," Raspal replied. "But this one time, and this one time only, I'm going to let you hold onto my tail. But if you pull it, I swear I'll bite you! And I mean it. Now—gently!—grab a hold."

Brett obediently did as he was told, and Raspal turned off his magic ball. Instantly, pitch-blackness covered them. Brett now followed the fox like a blind man follows his guide dog, and they traveled as fast as they could in the utter dark. Brett had no idea how Raspal could see in here.

After about a half-hour of travel, Brett got the sense that the tunnel walls had given way to a large opening, and he felt light breezes moving his hair. Raspal came to a sudden stop and stood stock-still. Brett had a sense of vastness all around him in the blackness.

"Something's not right," Raspal muttered. "I don't hear or smell anyone or anything, but I sense that magic is at work here. It feels like a masking. Like something's being hidden from me. What is going on?"

At that instant—almost like an answer to the fox's question—a bright light suddenly lit the cave around them, and for a moment, both Brett and Raspal were completely blinded. When his eyes had adjusted, Brett saw that he and the fox stood about fifty feet inside a huge cavern. It was easily three hundred yards across and a hundred feet high, and all around its circumference were countless tunnel entrances.

And out of these tunnel entrances were pouring thousands upon thousands of Gnomes.

In no time at all, they had Brett and Raspal completely surrounded and forced back against the cavern's wall.

"Driven by the hounds into the sights of the hunters," Raspal muttered with self-disgust under his breath. "I should have known better. After all, I am a fox!"

A tall Gnome with a flowing robe and Tanzalite encrusted crown stepped forward and regarded Brett and Raspal with disdain.

"So, you thought that you could sneak out of my Kingdom with my Grandfather's sword, did you?" he said. "How truly stupid of you, Raspal. I would have expected smarter from the Queen's own stooge. Now, you have only one option: willingly hand over Cabral's Sword and I will consider being lenient with you. Choose otherwise, and you will die sooner rather than later.

"And do not expect to defend yourself with our sword. It will not fight against Gnomes."

"Okay, King Calab," Raspal answered. "Here's the deal. I'd be willing to bet gold that the Sword's Elvish Magic will defend it's owner at all costs—but we really don't want trouble—so this is my offer to you. If you let us go, when we are done with our Quest of rebuilding the Northern Shield, and this boy-child returns to his world, the sword will no longer have an owner and I will personally see that it is restored to the Gnomes. I give you my word as a Courier of The Queen. And you know that she will honor my promise. My word is bond."

Calab thought about this for moment, all the while sizing Brett up and down, as if looking for weaknesses. One of his hands caressed a large Tanzalite stone set in a gold chain around his throat, while the other drummed nervously on his own sword's sheathed hilt. To Brett, he didn't seem very confident for a King.

"Whether or not your promise will be honored," he finally said, "is irrelevant. Even if I did trust you, too many things can happen if the Sword and its Stone leave my kingdom. Someone could capture it again, and once more the Gnomes would have no recourse. No. It is here now, and it will stay.

"You will either surrender our sword to us—or you will die!"

Raspal slipped back behind Brett's legs and up against the cave wall. "Your one chance to get your sword back is rapidly disappearing," the fox replied. "Change your mind before it's too late."

But the Gnome King simply took several steps backward himself, which was kind of cowardly, Brett thought, and let other Gnomes with drawn swords in front of him. The Sword of Cabral had now come fully to life in Brett's hands, its ruins flashing gold, its spell slowly settling down upon him. It was taking control, and even though it wasn't as aggressive and angry as it had been with the Lycants, it was still very stern and focused—much more so than it had been in the first fight with the Gnomes. It was almost as if the sheer number of the Gnomes was making it mad.

"Take him!" King Calab cried, and the small, wizened warriors closed in from all sides. Brett's blade became an instant blur of motion. It darted all around him, this way and that, in and out. And everywhere it went, the Gnomish blades either flew from the attackers hands or were shattered into flying shards of steel by the sheer force of the swords magic and Brett's defense.

But still the Gnomes pressed relentlessly forward, a new warrior replacing every one that was disarmed.

And now Brett felt his sword becoming angry. They could see that it would actually fight. They had been warned. And still they attacked. Suddenly, the Sword of Cabral changed its fighting style. Suddenly, it attacked back.

Now, Brett strode forward and more than just gnomish blades

went flying through the air. The Gnomes themselves were tossed as well. One, two, three. In less than a minute over ten little men were thrown aside. Seven limped or crawled away, but three of them lay in motionless piles.

Shocked and confused, the Gnomish army fell back. They stumbled over each other in their retreat. When they were well out of Brett's reach, they stopped and formed a half circle around him.

"The Sword has killed Gnomes," one of them exclaimed as a shocked murmuring ran through the crowd.

"This is not right," another said. "The Stone is ours. It is a part of us."

"I told you his sword would fight," Raspal said from behind Brett. "It is Elvish magic in that Stone, and it doesn't know the Gnomes. Now, I will extend my offer one more time. Let us go, and you have the Queen's own word that the sword will be returned when our quest is over!"

"And your offer will be refused one more time!" cried King Calab from safely in the rear. "Let us see how the boy does against stones!"

At that moment, a group of Gnomes rolled a huge boulder out of an adjacent tunnel. They steered it straight toward Raspal and Brett, and it picked up speed as it traveled. Two more boulders came out of two more entrances, and all three rolled straight toward them from different directions.

"This way, Brett," Raspal said. "We can't fight rolling rocks. We'll have to fight our way through the tunnels." And with that, the fox quickly darted into a small cave just to their left. Brett followed closely behind, all the while watching over his shoulder.

"Where does this go?" he asked as they ran.

"I don't know. I've never been down this one before. I guess we'll find out when we get there."

Right then, they came around a bend and came face to face with a blank stone wall. The tunnel was a dead end. Raspal muttered something under his breath and his brown magic-lights appeared all around.

"There's no hidden holes," he said. "Let's go back."

They turned and retraced their steps to the entrance, but it was now completely blocked by one of the huge boulders. Not so much as a single ray of light shone through the seal.

"I'm doing dreadful, aren't I?" Raspal muttered. "Outfoxed by a Gnome. I'll never live this down."

"What do we do now?" Brett asked.

"We wait," Raspal answered. "Unless you can move that stone, that is."

Being game for anything, Brett sheathed his sword and put his shoulder against the huge rock and pushed. It didn't even give a hint of moving. It was like pushing against a stone wall.

"Oh, don't bother, Brett. More than just the weight of that stone holds it. They've also cast a spell to seal it in place and cut off our air. They plan to suffocate us."

"How long will we last, do you think?"

"Twenty-four hours, maybe less," the fox answered. "But I'm just guessing, really. I've actually never been trapped like this before."

"Great," Brett muttered and plopped down on the ground. He leaned against the cave wall and stared bleakly at the floor. There really wasn't much that he could do. His sword was of no use now. Raspal came over and sat next to him. He wasn't nearly as cocky now, and he seemed a bit ashamed of himself.

"Don't lose hope, my boy," he said. "Remember, we still have a Blue Unicorn out there somewhere who will be looking for us.

"And with him is a young girl who is just brimming with magical power."

CHAPTER EIGHT

Magic to the Rescue

The day that Brett was busy running after Raspal and scrambling through dark, dirty tunnels and small caves, Alyssa was having a quiet horseback ride through the beautiful Starfire Mountains. These mountains, she found, were much greener and softer than the Rockroller Mountains had been. They were covered with thick stands of tall pines and groves of aspens, and the ground here was made of soft, sandy dirt with hardly a rock to be seen. The pack train followed a small, babbling stream upwards most of the day, which became smaller and smaller as they rode, until it was barely a trickle through stands of tall grass.

By mid-afternoon, they came to a high mountain meadow where the unicorn called for a break. Alyssa stretched her legs while Blue and the ponies spread out across the grass and began to graze. Blue hadn't spoken very much today—nor had anyone else for that matter—and to Alyssa, the entire group didn't seem to be very stressed at all. Except maybe Sturgill, who always seemed alert and a little on edge. Everyone else seemed to think that Brett was in good hands with Raspal, and it really was hard to imagine danger while riding through these peaceful mountains. Sturgill followed dutifully behind Alyssa as she walked through the grass in the meadow and looked at the wildflowers.

Suddenly, far in the distance, wolves began to yap and howl. Sturgill stiffened and cocked his head to one side, and after a moment, he howled in return.

"What's happening?" Alyssa asked. She was suddenly nervous—danger did seem to come out of nowhere here in Tanzal.

"The pack has found food," Sturgill answered. "They call me to eat, but I have told them that I cannot come."

"Oh," Alyssa sighed in relief. But then she quickly realized what the black wolf was talking about and wondered if something else was in danger. "What have they found?"

Sturgill glanced at her sideways, and the wolf seemed to be slightly amused by the question. "They are eating venison today," he answered evasively.

"You mean that they've killed a poor deer," she responded. "Just like my Dad and Brett are always doing every year on the deer hunt."

"Yes," the wolf answered. He still sounded amused, and not in the least bit remorseful. "They have caught a deer. A large, juicy buck to be exact. In order to live, Alyssa, everything must eat, and wolves do not apologize for loving their lives and wanting to continue to live. But remember this one thing about the Way of The Talking Wolves—unlike evil things, we always honor those who fall, be they wolf or deer. The life of the deer is as precious to us as is our own, because without each other, neither would live."

Alyssa nodded. She understood about predator and prey relationships, and she hadn't meant to sound judgmental, but apparently Sturgill had taken it that way. It was probably best just to leave things alone at this point, but Alyssa couldn't. She didn't like people—or a wolf in this case—to think that she was judgmental or snobbish.

"Well, we should eat, too," she said and she walked over to one of the grazing ponies and opened its pack. She pulled out some day-old bread and honey-butter as well as a bag of jerky. She gave a large handful of the jerky to Sturgill and then took a couple of pieces for herself. It was tough and chewy, but the flavor was very good—kind of sweet and spicy, like barbecue. The wolf seemed to smile as he watched her eat it.

"I see that you like venison as well," he said.

"Yes," she said. "I do. My dad goes hunting every year, and he almost always gets one, so we eat it at home all the time. Everyone must eat to live."

Sturgill chuckled wolfishly. "Indeed," he said between bites.

The two ate in silence for the next ten minutes, and when they were finished, Alyssa found a small trickle of water that was the beginnings of the stream and washed up. Sturgill leaned down next to her and took a drink of it.

"How long before we get going again?" she asked as she dried her hands and looked around. The ponies seemed to be bunching up again—like they were getting ready to go—but Blue was off at the edge of the meadow, gazing up at the distant peaks.

"I imagine very soon," Sturgill replied. "But, first, I think that there's something here that you and I need to do. Have you noticed that dead tree over there?"

Alyssa turned to look. At the edge of the clearing stood a tall, burned out stump. It looked like lightening had struck it several years before, splitting it down the center. Several blackened limbs lay on the ground around it, but none were left attached.

"Yeah," Alyssa said "What about it?"

"I think I see a robin nesting in it," the wolf replied.

Alyssa looked closer and saw what he was talking about. The center of the trunk had rotted away, creating a hollow spot, and she could just see a bird's head watching them through a crack in the front.

"I see it," she said as she walked over. The top of the old stump came to just below her nose, and by standing on her tiptoes she could easily see into the nest. The bird did indeed look like a robin—only it was the biggest robin she had ever seen. It was easily three times the size of a normal robin, about the size of a small chicken, and instead of the orangish-red colored breasts like the robins at home, this one's chest feathers were a bright, fire engine red. The bird cautiously watched her with large, solemn eyes.

"It is nesting," she said.

"How many eggs does she have?"

"I can't tell," Alyssa answered. But just then the bird stood and stepped to the side of the nest, showing a clutch of five, baby-blue eggs. They were the size of golf balls. "She has five. Why?"

Sturgill chuckled to himself. It was a rough, growling laugh that came from somewhere deep in his chest. He seemed extremely pleased for some reason.

"I thought as much," he said more to himself than Alyssa. "Well, since we're going to visit the Gnomes, a couple of eggs will definitely come in handy. Sort of persuade them to see things our way, if you catch my drift."

"Oh, I couldn't just take her eggs," Alyssa objected.

"It might be the difference between saving your brother and not saving him. I'll be honest with you, Alyssa, I don't have the same confidence in that shifty little fox that Blue does. He's not as clever as he thinks he is, and I've always said that one of these days his cockiness is going to catch up to him. Unfortunately, I have a feeling that that day has come and we're going to have to go in and rescue the both of them now. A couple of eggs will be the difference between a long, hard-fought battle with the Gnomes, or simply walking through deserted caves until we find them. Trust me, Alyssa, Gnomes are flat-out terrified of the very sight of eggs. You really need to take at least two."

Alyssa thought about this for a moment, realizing of course that Sturgill was right. The robin would still have three left, which was probably more than she needed, not to mention the fact that she could lay more. But, still, was it right to just take her eggs? They were, after all, hers and not Alyssa's property.

At that moment, however, the bird did something that ended Alyssa's internal debate. She reached down with her beak and gently nudged two of the eggs to the edge of the nest, almost as if she were offering them.

"I think she wants me to take them," Alyssa said. "Is she a talking bird?"

"No," Sturgill said. "Birds can't talk, but some of them do understand what we are saying. I believe that she may be one of those. Go ahead; take the eggs. And just remember, Alyssa, all good things in Tanzal have a great stake in seeing you and Blue succeed in this Quest. Already, Dark Magic from behind the broken shield begins to touch everything. I sense it daily. If you fail, her chicks will be born into a world much different than the one in which she lived her life."

Alyssa did as she was told and reached down and took the two eggs. She gently placed one in each of her front pockets. The two green gemstones that she had taken from the Norf's cave were in her right, front pocket and she took them out and put them in her back one so that they wouldn't break an egg. The robin settled back down on her remaining three eggs.

"What were those?" Sturgill asked, suddenly alert and staring at her back pocket.

"What?" Alyssa asked. "Those two stones? They're a couple of jewels that we found in the Norf's cave. Blue said that I could have them. Why?"

"May I see them?"

"Sure." Alyssa took them back out and held them in front of the wolf. In the sunlight, the faint green tint of the stones looked like a reflection of the meadow grass all around them. Sturgill first sniffed and then nudged the two marble-sized gems.

"What you have there is two, very large Virgin Tanzalite stones!" he declared in surprise. "They are cut and ready for magic, but don't even have the slightest spell inside them. Two virgin stones these sizes are worth a king's ransom. People have been killed for smaller gems than these! Keep them safely out of sight."

"What's Tanzalite?" Alyssa asked.

"A gem that holds magic," Sturgill said. "Once cast, it's magic will never fade or need to regenerate after use, like magic in living beings does. But those stones have no magic; you can tell by their light color. Plus, I sensed into them. Stones with good magic turn dark green when they're full. Stones with evil magic go black. Some stones have both kinds of magic, and those are extremely dangerous to use. Only experienced magicians should touch them."

"Why would Blue let me have something so valuable?" she asked in sudden wonder as she rolled them around in the palm of her hand

and marveled at them. They now appeared all that much more beautiful. "I had no idea what they were when I asked for them. I thought that they were very light colored emeralds."

"Because I had a feeling that they came to you for a reason," said a voice directly behind Alyssa. She jumped in surprise and turned to find the unicorn standing there. "The same as Brett's sword and the Fourth Book of Magic. Out of all the jewels in the Norf's bag, you took the only two Virgin Tanzalites there. There's a reason for that. I just don't know what it is. Only time will tell.

"Now, speaking of time, lunch is over and we need to be going."

Blue whinnied and the ponies came and stood in their line behind him. Alyssa first checked all their saddles and then climbed up into her own. The procession then set off toward the distant peaks that the unicorn had been staring at.

The group climbed throughout the afternoon, higher and higher. The air grew thinner as they went and a cool, almost cold, breeze picked up and blew against Alyssa's back. Thick, dark clouds began to form on the western horizon, blocking out the lowering sun, while large white ones raced across the sky overhead.

"It might rain tonight," Sturgill muttered to himself. "We'll have to find trees to camp under. I don't think that they packed a tent."

As they neared the top of the mountain, the trail became extremely steep and rocky, and the small ponies had a hard time, laboring up slowly with the heavy packs. But they didn't seem to mind; just following a unicorn seemed to give them all the strength they needed.

The sun sank behind the distant hills as they crested the pass, and the pack train now had to pick its way back down in a growing gloom. By the time they reached the tree level again, it was full night, and Alyssa was forced to unsaddle the ponies and roll out her sleeping quilt in the dark. She was too tired to dig out any dinner, and simply crawled into her bag and fell asleep.

The last thing she remembered was Sturgill's weight on her blanket and his deep, even breathing as the big, black wolf curled up next to her.

* * *

When Alyssa felt Sturgill gently pawing at her, it startled her, and she came awake with a sudden jolt and half jumped out of her bed. "What's wrong?" she asked, looking hurriedly around.

"Nothing," Sturgill replied. "It's just time to get going."

Alyssa realized that the eastern horizon was just starting to brighten, and so settled back down. It wasn't night anymore; it was dawn. She felt like she hadn't gotten any sleep at all.

Great, she thought. *Another fun-filled day of riding horses.*

Alyssa rubbed the sleep from her eyes and chuckled at herself. There had been a time—about, oh, a week or so ago—when she had thought that she could never get enough of horseback riding. She had always been *sooo* jealous of Katie and her 4H horse group. Now, even though she wasn't quite as stiff and sore as yesterday morning, she was ready to take a turn at walking behind the ponies. A day of hiking and climbing sounded like relaxation at this point. Especially climbing.

But she didn't think that Blue would let her. His attitude was very different this morning, and he seemed anxious to go. He was walking slowly back and forth in camp, almost like a lion pacing his pen. And even though Alyssa ate her breakfast and saddled the ponies as fast as she could, she sensed that Blue was itching to help her, but couldn't. His four hooves might be able to send him racing across the ground like the wind, but they weren't much use in tying cinches. One of the good things about getting Brett back was that she would have help with the saddles again.

About the time that Alyssa was finished, the sun was just starting to lift itself above the mountains to the east. Its rays shone through a patchwork of thick, grey clouds. It hadn't rained last night, but the clouds were still building. A strong, wet-smelling breeze blew from the west.

After checking her cinch a second time, Alyssa started to climb onto her pony.

"No, Alyssa," Blue said. "You'll be riding me today. I will

probably need your magic against the Gnomes when we go in after your brother and Raspal."

At this, Sturgill cocked his head at gazed sideways over at the unicorn. His face held a slightly surprised, but amused, look on it.

"So you think that we'll have to go in, do you?" he asked with a light laugh.

"It wouldn't surprise me," Blue answered as Alyssa climbed onto his back. "In fact, Sturgill, I would be more surprised if Raspal was actually able to sneak them out all the way by himself. The Treestone Mine entrance is heavily guarded. I know that you don't care for him, but to perfectly honest with you, he was—and still is—my only hope. There is no way that I could go to where the boy fell. The tunnels that deep in the mountain are too narrow and too low for me to navigate. My only hope is that they'll reach a place close enough to the outside entrance that Alyssa and I can reach them.

"If Raspal can just accomplish that," Blue finished, his voice becoming low and grim. "Trust me, I'll do the rest. And the Gnome King will find out what it means to face a Blue Unicorn that is on his Quest!"

The wolf still didn't seem all that impressed, and he muttered something Alyssa didn't fully catch, but it sounded like something about how a dozen wolves and a couple eggs would do the trick just as well—if not better. But, despite his grumblings, Sturgill dutifully fell into step alongside Blue as they started down the trail. Apparently, he was still guarding her even though she was riding the unicorn.

After about a half-hour of quick travel, several wolves howled in the distance, first one in the east, then two in to the North and one in the west. Sturgill stopped and cocked an ear.

"What do they say?" Blue asked.

"That all aboveground Gnome activity has stopped overnight," Sturgill answered. "There's no sign of them anywhere. That's the bad news. The good news is that there's also no sign of any more Lycants or Trolls. We'll have at least a couple of days of clear travel."

"Sturgill, call your pack in," Blue grimly ordered. "The Gnomes have surely discovered the boy and what sword he carries. That's why they've all gone underground. Nothing but the Sword of Cabral would draw the entire Kingdom. We must move fast. Have them meet us near the mine entrance as quickly as they can. And tell them to be ready for battle!"

Sturgill sat on his haunches, lifted his snout upward and howled loudly into the morning sky. His voice rang out deep and commanding, and even though it was a howl and not words, Alyssa could hear the sense of urgency and excitement in it. Blue whinnied back at the ponies, and then jumped forward and broke into a full run. His mane blew wildly in the stiff wind as he raced down the trail. Alyssa buried her face in the bottom of it to keep it from whipping her eyes. All around her, some very close, some much farther away, she could hear Sturgill's pack answering him. They all sounded full of energy and excitement. That was wolves for you, Alyssa figured—always spoiling for a good fight.

"The ponies know the way," Blue said over his shoulder as he ran. "I have told them to meet us later. It's actually best if we're alone. We are going to have quite a battle on our hands, what with the entire Gnome army standing against us. We're going to be outnumbered by at least a thousand to one. Lucky for us we have your magic."

And eggs, too, Alyssa thought.

The unicorn ran for only another twenty minutes before the trail leveled out and widened considerably. He now slowed his pace and watched around them. Here, over the long years, hundreds of feet had pounded the soil into dust and trampled even the most daring of weeds into nothingness. Alyssa noticed that many of the trees on both sides of what was quickly becoming a road, were dead but still standing, and that they were a strange color of blackish brown streaked with grey. Quite a few had fallen and broken into sharp shapes, almost like shattered stones.

Petrified wood, she suddenly realized. They were traveling through an ancient petrified forest. She now saw piles of petrified wood all around. It literally littered the ground, and the farther they went, the fewer live trees there were. Of course, she thought to herself, this was the Treestone Mine, and that's what petrified wood was—Treestone. It all made perfect sense.

Blue now came to a full stop, and sniffed the air around them. He seemed irritated at something and pawed the ground.

"They've retreated to the mine," Sturgill stated in a matter-of-fact type of voice. He had easily kept pace during the run and now stood alongside Blue and was sniffing the air as well. Eight of his pack flanked him, and more wolves, some in pairs and some alone, were materializing out from between the stone trees every few minutes or so.

"Yes, they have," Blue agreed as he turned slowly around, his nose held high. "And I feel a sudden sense of urgency, too. They've done something. I can feel it. It feels like the air is getting close and tight. We must move—and now!"

The Unicorn abruptly wheeled and trotted down the road. His gait was high and tight, his neck held stiff. Alyssa could sense the tension in all his muscles. He was like a coiled spring beneath her. At this moment, she was glad that she wasn't a Gnome, especially when she glanced back and saw that the pack of wolves had grown to over twenty. They were shadowy shapes trailing silently along behind them.

Rounding a bend in the road, the group came face to face with a sheer cliff wall and the entrance to the Treestone Mine. The mine's doors were hewn from what looked to Alyssa like two, single pieces of solid black and white granite, and stood in sharp contrast to the red sandstone of the cliff's walls. They were an easy ten feet tall and curved at the top to fit snugly into the mine's arched tunnel. Ancient ruins and carvings of petrified trees had been etched into both the door's granite and the soft sandstone around it. In a strange way, it reminded Alyssa of the Indian Petroglyphs she often found while climbing on the red cliffs down in Arches and Canyonlands National park.

In front of the stone doors, stood four Gnome guards—who didn't look at all pleased to see a unicorn and pack of wolves suddenly appear at their doorstep. Two stepped nervously from one foot to the other, while the other two fingered their sheathed swords. To Alyssa, they seemed very upset about something, maybe even guilty. None of them appeared to know what to do.

Finally, a younger and not quite as wizened Gnome stepped forward. He nervously caressed a very small, dark green stone hung on a silver chain around his neck. Apparently, he was in charge.

"We are not open today," he finally squeaked, and Alyssa almost laughed at the sound of his voice, but barely managed to choke it back. He sounded like a scared five-year-old who had just been caught taking a breath from a helium balloon.

"We're conducting Private Gnome Kingdom business today," he finished lamely.

"I will see the gatekeeper," Blue replied. His voice was low and ominous. "And I will not be denied."

The young Gnome nervously shifted his weight back and forth, and his hand gripped his sword handle so tight that his wrinkled skin turned an even paler shade of white.

"I'm sorry," he stammered. "I have my orders. No one goes in today."

Blue seemed to suddenly grow, and it seemed to Alyssa like she was now farther from the ground. She could almost feel his anger and power welling up inside him. His horn turned bright silver and flashed with streaks of blue, while his hooves began to glow like heated steel.

"I will give you one more chance," he replied in a soft but deadly voice. "Open the way and allow me to see the gatekeeper, or I will go through you, reduce your gates to rubble and allow my wolves to feast on what I leave behind."

Sturgill and several of the larger wolves growled ominously for effect and crept forward, their bellies low to the ground.

The small man almost jumped out of his tunic in fright.

"Open the gate!" he squealed as he turned and ran toward the doors. "Let the gatekeeper deal with this!"

The four Gnomes pushed the stone doors open and ran inside.

Blue slowly followed, watching cautiously all around him. He was ready for anything, including an ambush.

The first section of the Treestone Mine was a large, open cavern. It was about thirty feet deep, a hundred feet long and over twenty feet high. Its walls were made of the same red sandstone as outside, and it was lit by at least a hundred, smokeless torches tucked into small alcoves all around its walls and ceilings. Three smaller tunnels that led off from the main cavern were guarded by a half-dozen warriors each, all of whom now had their swords drawn.

In the center of this room stood a large, white marble desk. The old Gnome sitting behind it seemed a great deal more calm and collected than the young guard from the gate, who was now standing before him and feverishly explaining to him what had happened.

With a contemptuous snort the Gatekeeper waved the guard aside and pulled a large, leather-bound book toward him. He opened it and began to thumb through it, as if looking for something. It wasn't until Blue had stepped to within a foot of him that he finally glanced up. He appraised the unicorn up and down, his gaze steely and unflinching.

"You were advised that we are closed for business today," he finally said, his voice fairly dripping with contempt. "But you insisted on coming in anyway, so I have done you the courtesy of checking for appointments. I found none. Not for a unicorn, nor for," he now gazed with disdain toward Sturgill and his crouching pack, "any other *things.*

"Now, please remove yourself from the premises or else I will be forced to do it physically. And, please, take those mangy animals with you!"

At this, Sturgill growled deep in his chest, and Blue glanced down at him to caution him back. The black wolf's eyes shone with murder, but he held himself in check.

"I have no appointment, nor do I need one," Blue said in a soft but deadly voice. Alyssa could tell that he was nearing the end of his patience. "I am here for the fox and the young boy that fell into one of your traps. Now tell me where they are."

"I have no idea what you're talking about," the gatekeeper exclaimed, but his eyes shone with sudden surprise before he quickly dropped them to the book in front of him.

Without another word, or warning of any kind, the unicorn reared up. His front hooves flashed with fire and lightening. He brought them crashing down on the center of the marble desk. With a clap of thunder, it broke into five large pieces. The old Gnome screamed in fright and surprise as he fell backwards. A large section of marble fell on his right arm, pinning him to the ground.

Blue stepped forward and used his left hoof to pin the Gatekeeper's other arm to the ground as well. He then bent his head and placed the tip of his horn directly over the Gnome's wildly beating heart.

"You have one chance left," he said quietly. "Tell me where the fox and the young boy are or I will skewer you like meat on a grillstick and then I will go find another Gnome and give to him this exact same choice. I will do this until I get what I came here for, or until I run out of Gnomes, whichever comes first. Now, it is time for you to choose!"

"It will do you no good," the gatekeeper squeaked. His aura of contempt, along with all his guards, had suddenly evaporated. "The King and his entire army are guarding them. They are to be punished for trespassing."

Blue pushed down on his horn's tip. It poked a small hole in the fabric of the little man's white robe.

"Tell me quick," he murmured. "My patience wanes and your time grows short. If I need to find another Gnome, I will. Where is the boy and the fox?"

"They're in the Amphitheater," he cried in terror. "It's about a hundred yards down the far left corridor."

"Thank you," Blue replied. He lifted his glowing horn and took a step back. "Sturgill, assign one of your 'mangy animals' to sit on him until we return. If he has lied to us, when I come back through, he will have my permission to eat him."

Sturgill silently nodded toward a large gray wolf, who gleefully climbed onto the Gatekeeper's chest. Blue then wheeled and trotted toward the far tunnel. Sturgill and his pack followed behind.

The last thing Alyssa saw over her shoulder was that the gray wolf had lain down on the pinned Gnome's body and was gently licking the side of the old man's face.

The tunnel leading to the Amphitheater was tall and wide. Its floor was covered wall-to-wall with close-fitting, flat stones, and to Alyssa it looked like two horses pulling carts could go through it side by side. That was probably exactly what it was for, she figured. They had gone only a short distance before they saw a large group of armed Gnomes standing directly in their path. It looked like about hundred or so, and they backed away as Blue advanced on them.

When they reached the end of the tunnel, the contingent of Gnome warriors moved slowly backwards into a huge, underground cavern. Alyssa couldn't tell if this vast cave was natural or Gnome-made, but it was an easy three football fields long, four football fields wide, and its ceiling was at least a hundred feet high.

And it was completely filled with Gnome soldiers, every one of whom were armed to the teeth.

Blue moved fearlessly into this underground amphitheater and stopped ten feet from the nearest warrior. He gazed slowly around himself until he spotted what he was looking for.

"There you are, my dear Calab," he said. The unicorn's voice was calm and even, almost as if he were making conversation at a party. "How nice to see you again. How are things going? I hear the mining's gone well this year."

A tall Gnome about twenty soldiers back nervously returned Blue's gaze. In his hands he held a Tanzalite-encrusted, golden scepter instead of a sword, and Alyssa figured that he was someone important because he also wore a large, jeweled crown. The space in a circle around him for about ten feet was empty, except for two large—well, large for Gnomes that is, which is to say that they were almost Brett's size—bodyguards. He seemed extremely displeased with the unicorn's presence.

"Things were better a moment ago," he answered, sounding very irritated. "Blue, you've broken into my Kingdom, done unauthorized magic and violence, and now address me as if you were an invited guest at a tea party. You know that because you are The Blue Unicorn, I have always held you in the greatest esteem, but this is unwarranted. Tell me what you want, and then be gone."

"You know what I want," Blue replied softly. Alyssa could sense his power starting to grow again. It was like sitting on a ticking bomb. "I am here for Raspal and the boy with him. You caught them in one of your traps. Release them now, or I will take them. I sense that their time, as well as their air, grows short."

"I will not!" King Calab answered defiantly. "They possess something very valuable of mine and have refused to give it to me willingly. Now, they can never leave!"

Blue lowered his horn slightly, giving just a hint of a threat. It had started to glow again.

"Take caution, Calab," he said ominously. "And think your decision all the way through. I don't want trouble with the Gnomes, but I will do what I have to do. Remember, I *am* The Blue Unicorn, and I now give you fair warning: I have embarked upon The Unicorn's Quest, and the boy is essential to it. I will take both him and that fox with me—or die trying!"

"Then it is time for you to die!" Calab yelled. "And your Quest be hanged as well as you! Attack them, men! Take them all!"

In a rush, the Gnome army surged forward. They were met with a unicorn's furiously swinging horn and flashing hooves. Swords, shields and Gnomes flew in all directions. The stunned soldiers fell back for a moment, and in that instant, Blue reared, neighing loudly. He then brought his front feet crashing down onto the ground in front of him. A large crack appeared in the rock under his hooves and the entire cavern shook like an earthquake had hit it. Most of the Gnome army, as well as some of Sturgill's pack, lost their footing and tumbled to the ground. Dust and rocks rained down from the ceiling above.

With all his hooves now flashing fire and lightening, Blue charged forward. He went through the little men like a bowling ball through pins, and Alyssa could hear the wolf pack fighting and growling viciously behind her. She should help, she thought, and soon. What was the point of bringing eggs and not using them when the time finally came?

As Blue reared up and down, striking out in all directions, Alyssa grabbed his mane with one hand and used her other to reach into her front pocket. It took all her concentration—as well as Blue's magic—just for her to stay on his back. Finally, she was able to pull one free.

But at that instant, the unicorn whirled under her, and Alyssa lost her grip on the egg.

It went sailing through the air.

And hit a young Gnome warrior squarely on the forehead.

Alyssa saw him reach up and pull a handful of broken yolk and eggshell from out of his eyes. The young soldier stared at it in complete horror.

The scream he then gave out was the most bloodcurdling thing that Alyssa had ever heard.

"EGGS!" he cried in total terror. "She has eggs! *And she's throwing them!* I've been hit! I've been hit! And now I'm going to grow old! And die!"

At this, the entire Gnome army froze in its tracks. This was just too much for them. They were facing a ravenous wolf pack, a Thundering Unicorn—and now flying *Eggs* as well? Almost as one, the army turned and ran for the closest cave or tunnel leading out of the Amphitheater.

"No!" screamed King Calab. "They can't have very many. Come back and fight. I order you to! *They have Cabral's Sword!* And they will take it with them. We'll never have a chance like this again!"

But his yelling was of absolutely no use. The Gnome army was done fighting for the day. They would face anything for the Sword of Cabral—except eggs!

In no time at all, only King Calab and his two large bodyguards were left to fight the Unicorn.

With Sturgill at his heels, Blue advanced slowly on the

threesome, his horn held low. Alyssa reached into her other pocket and pulled out the second Robin's egg.

At the sight of the baby blue egg, both of Calab's guards turned and ran. Calab squealed in terror himself, whirled around and followed right behind.

Apparently, he was done fighting as well.

Blue now glanced back at Alyssa. His eyes were still spinning with the excitement of battle, but he also seemed a bit irritated.

"I didn't know that you had eggs," he said. "You probably should have told me. Where did you get them?"

"I'm sorry," Alyssa said. "I meant to, but then I forgot. We got talking about Tanzalite, and then it slipped my mind. I really am sorry."

"But where did you get them?" Blue asked again.

"Sturgill found them," Alyssa answered. "He spotted a Robin's nest."

"Oh, I see," Blue said. He glanced in irritation over at Sturgill, who was now sitting on his haunches and licking a small wound on his front paw. The black wolf was also trying his best not to smile in amusement, and he had a self-satisfied but guilty air about him, like the wolf who had just got caught finishing off the farmer's prize pig.

"It must have slipped my mind as well," he said casually. "But you have to admit; it was a pleasant surprise!"

"For future reference, Sturgill," Blue said. "I prefer *not* to have 'pleasant surprises'."

"I'll keep that in mind," the wolf assured him with a smile.

Without another word, Blue turned and trotted across the now empty Amphitheater. He walked straight toward the far wall. As they approached, Alyssa could see that the cave in front of them had been blocked up with a huge boulder. It was at least as tall as Blue and three times as wide. The unicorn put his nose directly on this stone and his blue magic-lights suddenly appeared all around them.

After a moment, he took a step backward, and his lights disappeared.

"It's as I feared," he said with a sigh. "The Gnomes have sealed it with magic—very strong magic, for Gnomes. And the air inside is running out. I don't have time to finesse the series of spells needed to open it slowly. I'm going to have to crush the boulder with pure force, and at the same time, destroy their Sealing Spell.

"Alyssa, I'm afraid that I'm going to need to use your magic again."

"I don't mind," she replied cheerfully.

Blue sighed in resignation and shook his head. "I know you don't," he said "But I do. Every time I use that much sheer power at once, anyone attuned to magic can sense it—including Lord Falgerth. It's like screaming 'Here I am!' But I can't see any other way around it. You'll have to put your hands on my neck."

Alyssa did as Blue asked and waited. It was only a moment before she felt herself connecting with him and her magic being slowly pulled out of her. The now familiar magic-trance fell upon on her; it was so much like being in a waking dream, she thought to herself.

Suddenly, Blue reared beneath her.

"Anonis il Separis!" he cried, bringing his front hooves crashing down on the boulder's side. They struck with an incredibly loud boom, like the loudest clap of thunder Alyssa had ever heard.

For just an instant, nothing happened. But then a small spider web of cracks appeared in the boulder directly under Blue's hooves. They slowly spread out in all directions across the stone.

Then, without any warning, the huge rock simply collapsed into a cloud of rock dust and a pile of sand. The suddenness of it caught Alyssa off guard, and it surprised her that it had fallen into sand. She had expected too see it crumble into gravel like the wall in the Norf's cave had done. Blue must have also used a stronger spell. He did seem to be running out of patience. Alyssa's magic trance disappeared as the connection between her and the unicorn was broken.

"What's done is done," Alyssa heard Blue mutter to himself under his breath.

A set of pointy ears now appeared in the newly made opening above the sand. They were quickly followed the rest of Raspal's familiar outline. Brett scrambled out right behind him. Alyssa was extremely relived to see that he was fine—despite all his faults and smart aleck remarks, she did love him.

"Thanks," Brett panted as he climbed down the pile. "Man, it was getting hot in there. I'm telling you, Lyssa, I think we were running out of air. You came just in time. Thank you so much!"

"Yes," Raspal agreed. "Thank you. And that is meant for all of you—even you, Sturgill. I owe you one."

Sturgill grumbled something under his breath that Alyssa didn't catch, but she could see that the wolf was pleased with this admission. Apparently, it hadn't been expected.

"Our greetings will have to wait," Blue said impatiently. "We are still in the Gnome Kingdom. Quickly, Brett, climb up and let's go. Our time is short."

Brett did as he was told, and Alyssa could see by the way he easily jumped on that he wasn't hurt, which she was also glad for.

"Boy, do I have some stuff to tell you," he whispered in her ear as he wrapped his arms around her stomach. "There's a lot more stuff going on here than you know! And those Gnomes want my sword bad."

"I already figured that out," Alyssa whispered back as Blue turned and trotted rapidly back the way he had come. She got the feeling from his quick and determined stride that there was nothing on Tanzal that could stop him from getting out now.

Nothing even tried.

When they reached the mine entrance, Sturgill called the gray wolf off the Gatekeeper. He seemed disappointed that he didn't get to eat the little man, but did as he was told.

"Let me have your last egg," Sturgill said to Alyssa as they exited the mine. "I have a little plan for it."

Alyssa leaned down and the wolf took it gently in his mouth.

The last she saw of the Treestone Mine was Sturgill placing the Robin's egg in the cave's open doorway.

It would be days before the Gnomes screwed up the courage to move it, he told her later that night. Literally days.

They were not in any danger of being followed now, Sturgill proclaimed with amusement to everyone as he caught up with the group.

"No," Blue replied in a very grim voice as he trotted along. "Maybe not from Gnomes. But Lord Falgerth now knows exactly where we are. Send your scouts back out, Sturgill, because I'm sure that more Lycants and Trolls will be coming.

"And this time, he'll send enough to do the job right. We'll be outnumbered by a long ways. I have no doubt about it."

CHAPTER NINE

Ghosts and Shadows

Outside the mine, the group traveled quickly back down the trail leading up to the entrance. Brett marveled at the still standing petrified trees, and even pointed out several that had branches with twigs attached, but Alyssa didn't pay much attention. She'd seen this before. Her mind was still whirling from the rescue. Things had happened with such lightening speed.

They hadn't gone far before they came across the ponies grazing quietly in a small clearing among the mounds of several tumbled down petrified trees. Blue whinnied at them, and they looked up, whinnied back and then calmly returned to chomping grass. To Alyssa, they didn't seem the least bit stressed. The ponies had absolute faith in the unicorn's leadership, and she was beginning to see why.

"Time for lunch," Blue said. "But let's make it a quick one. We need to move again, and soon."

Brett and Alyssa slid off the unicorn's back and walked over to the pony with the food pack on. Alyssa rummaged around until she found the jerky, then took a large handful of it and set it on the ground in front of Sturgill, who had dutifully followed her over. She then found some biscuits and apples for her and Brett.

From the edge of the clearing, two gray wolves barked at Sturgill. He barked in return, and then the entire pack melted magically into the forest.

"Where are they going?" Brett asked.

"To find lunch as well," Sturgill said. "And then go scouting." He picked up a piece of the jerky and chewed on it. A few minutes later, in the distance a chorus of yips and barks filled the air. Sturgill cocked his ear and then smiled in amusement.

"What's that about?" Alyssa asked.

"My pack is making fun of me," he said, sounding just a touch annoyed. "They say that I've been domesticated. And that I'm no better than a house dog being fed by its master."

"I'm sorry," Alyssa said, feeling suddenly horrible. "I didn't even think about that! I didn't mean it that way."

"Of course you didn't," Sturgill answered "And believe me, it's not a problem. They're just joking around. You notice that they asked for my permission to leave, and only teased me when they were safely away?"

The black wolf's eyes suddenly shone fiercely, and his voice took on a steely tone when he continued, "That's because they all know that I'm far from tame, and anyone standing a little too close when he says otherwise might loose some fur – and *fast!*"

The wolf chuckled to himself and went back to eating jerky. Brett took a piece as well and chomped quickly on it, acting almost as if he needed something to do. His movements were quick and impatient, and his eyes spun with excitement.

Ever since they'd rescued him and Raspal, Alyssa had thought that Brett was acting funny. During the ride out, she'd simply shrugged it off as a reaction to being trapped by the Gnomes, but now she was starting to wonder. She knew Brett well—had known him all his life in fact—and she could tell that he had a secret that he was just bursting at the seams to tell to her. But he also wanted to keep it because it made him feel superior. Alyssa wasn't going to ask him what it was—she wouldn't give him the satisfaction. Anyways, he'd tell her soon enough on his own. His record for keeping a secret was, oh, about, maybe five minutes.

And of course, Alyssa was once again right.

"Did you know that Blue is not a normal unicorn," he mentioned casually between bites on his jerky.

"Of course he's not," Sturgill interrupted, glancing up. "He's The Blue Unicorn. That the most not normal a unicorn can get."

"He's like what a White Buffalo is to the Indians," Brett added quickly, cutting the wolf off. Apparently, he had his whole speech planned out and wasn't going to let Sturgill tell it for him—he had never been one to let someone else steal his thunder.

In a very excited voice, Brett re-told Alyssa everything that Raspal had told him the night before. He told her all about the Three Silver Sentinels, The Blue Unicorn, The Unicorn's Quest and even about Tanzalite—some of which she already knew from Sturgill—and his sword's special stone.

When he was done, Alyssa sat and quietly thought about all of this. She had always had an inkling by the way everyone treated him that there was something special about Blue—other than being a unicorn, of course—but she'd had no idea that it was this big. Apparently, he was an incredibly magical creature, even by Tanzal's standards.

Things were definitely getting curiouser and curiouser.

"And guess what his Unicorn's Quest is?" Brett asked with a tone of superiority.

"Helping me rebuild the Northern Shield?" Alyssa responded. "Making sure that I get there safely?"

"How did you know?" Brett's voice held a hurt tone to it.

"It's just obvious, isn't it?"

"I'm sorry, Alyssa," Sturgill said, interrupting them again. "I just assumed that you knew all of this. Everyone in Tanzal does, so I didn't even think that you might not. But of course you don't; you're not from Tanzal."

Alyssa didn't respond to this. Right now, she was feeling a little overwhelmed by everything and didn't want to talk. She took another bite of biscuit and fished out some deer jerky for herself as well. She had never been one to do anything important without a plan, not even her homework, but this was different from anything she'd ever done before. Everything felt so out of control. She didn't even know where they were going—it was someplace "North", everyone told her—

and she didn't know what she was supposed to do when she got there. Did she have to do magic? Or would Blue do it by simply pulling it out of her again, like he always did? Also, what was the Fourth Book of Magic for? And how could anyone know what it contained if up till now it had only been a legend? This was the one thing that was really starting to irritate her: No one was telling her what was going on!

Alyssa had a sinking feeling that it was because no one else really knew. She pulled out a juice skin and uncorked it, taking a small drink.

"Oh, my heck!" Brett suddenly said, pointing back toward the trail. "Who's that over there?"

Both Alyssa and Sturgill looked up, and for a brief moment, Alyssa felt a sudden sense of shock at what she saw. A man was standing at the edge of the clearing. A real, large-as-life human man. It was the first genuine person—other than the Queens floating "ghost"—that they'd seen since coming to Tanzal.

He was a tall, thin man, easily over six feet, and he had long, brown hair which was pulled away from his face and tied back with a leather strapping into a ponytail. His nose was long and sharp, his chin short and pointed and his high cheekbones stood out prominently on his thin, dark-skinned face. To Alyssa, he looked like a human hawk. He was dressed in a flowing, dark-blue robe and in his left hand he held a gnarled walking staff. Alyssa saw that a large, blackish gemstone was embedded into the top of it.

With a cold, contemptuous smile on his face, the man stepped between two piles of petrified wood and walked toward them.

"Lord Falgerth!" Sturgill growled angrily. "How could he get so close without me hearing? Hang my inattention! Blue, the enemy is among us! We are under attack!"

Growling ferociously, Sturgill crept slowly forward. His belly was low to the ground and the hackles on the back of his neck stood straight up. His movements were tight and tense, like a coiled spring. Brett pulled his sword free and followed right behind.

Lord Falgerth laughed out loud at the their advance, and he lifted his right hand and ran his thumb across the tips of his four fingers, starting with his pinky and ending with his index. When he was done, his hand clenched into a fist and black magic lights danced all around it.

The ground directly beneath both Sturgill and Brett suddenly sparkled and shimmered. It became semi-liquid, shining like glitter-filled quicksand, and the wolf sank into it up to his belly and chest, while Brett sank to his waist.

Falgerth's hand made the motion again, touching all his fingertips and then clenching into a fist. The magic lights sparkled once more, and the earth returned to its solid state. Both Brett and the black wolf were now trapped in the earth.

"I love doing that," Lord Falgerth said with a chuckle. "Even when it is completely unnecessary—like today!"

In a total frenzy, Sturgill began to growl and chew at the ground holding his front legs frozen. Dirt, as well as small bits of his fur, flew furiously in all directions. It was almost as if he thought he could dig himself out with just his teeth.

Brett simply stared down in awe.

"That's a pretty cool trick," he muttered under his breath. "I wish I could do it." He re-sheathed his sword and reached down to feel around his pant legs, just to make that he was actually buried.

Alyssa had no idea what she should do now. At that moment, she heard a footstep behind her and turned to find both Blue and Raspal had come up.

"Calm yourself, Sturgill," Blue said quietly. "Even if you could get out, which you can't, there's nothing that you could do. He's not actually here. He's ghosting. That's why you didn't hear him approach."

"Bravo for The Blue Unicorn!" Lord Falgerth exclaimed, clapping his hands and laughing. "One brain among you is better than none! I hate it when things are too easy."

Sturgill stopped tearing at the ground and stared intently at Falgerth. "He can't be ghosting," he objected. "He's much too solid, and he's walking. Anyways, he's not a "Ghoster", and never has been. He doesn't have the power."

"He does now," Blue replied softly.

"Indeed, my dear unicorn," Falgerth said. His tone had suddenly gone deadly serious and his eyes shone with a sudden hate. It sent a chill down Alyssa's spine. "I now wield a power that most Mages only dream about—Power long kept from Tanzal but that has now returned, and is in full, dark flower. You thought that by eliminating the Norfs, you dealt me a grievous blow, but the exact opposite is true. Atticus' sources of power could serve only one master, and with him gone, they gladly serve a new one. What doesn't kill you only makes you stronger!"

Falgerth's hand again made its quick motion, and the ground beneath Blue's feet shimmered and shone as it turned into magic quicksand.

But the unicorn didn't sink. Instead, he walked slowly forward toward Sturgill and Brett, his hooves glowing magically on top of the glittering earth.

"Save your cheap parlor tricks for someone else," Blue said with contempt. "If you wish magical battle, Falgerth, then by all means attack. Take your best shot. I stand eager and ready for you. I will put your stone statue next to Atticus' in my future retirement pasture. Otherwise, be gone with you, vile ghost."

As Blue passed between Brett and Sturgill, the liquid earth followed him and surrounded them. They took the opportunity to pull themselves out of the quickdirt and onto solid ground.

"You'd like that, wouldn't you?" Falgerth replied. "But only a idiot attacks while ghosting, and both of us know it. No, I'm here to save you a great deal of trouble, Blue. You are a fool on a fool's errand, sent by another fool, the Queen herself. Balance has returned to Tanzal, and it is here to stay. The Northern Shield cannot be rebuilt—I've destroyed even its foundation. Maybe the Ancient One could do it if he were alive today, but even his bones have turned to dust ages ago. You waste your time, and probably your life as well."

Blue snorted in anger and threw his head, like a stallion about to fight. His horn now glowed even brighter. It sent off several magical sparks.

"Both are mine to waste," he retorted. "And if you truly believed that, you would have never come. Save your simple lies and your childish manipulations for the imbeciles that you surround yourself with!"

The unicorn then lifted his right hoof and brought it down hard on the ground beneath him. It sounded like a large rock striking the earth, and the magical quickdirt instantly disappeared. Blue's magic lights now appeared around his shining horn. He looked like he was preparing to attack.

"Take care, fool!" Falgerth growled as he wrapped his cloak around his staff. "I have had a vision, and my visions always come true. In it, you are bitted, shackled and lying in defeat on a field of battle—and I am cutting your horn from your living head! I plan on hanging it from my dining room wall! Imagine that, owning the horn of a Blue Unicorn. Farewell, my arrogant friend!"

And in a flash of black magic lights, Falgerth disappeared.

Blue stamped his hoof again and snorted toward where he had been.

"I have had a vision as well," he said quietly to the now empty clearing. "And my visions also always come true. In it, at the edge of an old, dark forest, your life comes to an end on the tip of my undamaged horn."

Blue now turned to Alyssa. He was smiling and his eyes danced in amusement. "We can't both be right," he said to her with a laugh. "Now can we?"

"No," Alyssa answered hesitantly, not really knowing what to say. "I guess not."

"I'm sorry, blue," Sturgill said. "I shouldn't have lost my composure, but I honestly thought that he was here. I've never seen anyone ghost so strongly. He actually looked like he was *walking!*"

Blue glanced over at the wolf and nodded. "I understand," he said. "He was showing off his newfound power, and trying to scare me. He also wanted for us to see the new stone that he carries in his staff. It is very large and very powerful. I wonder where he got it from."

Now that Blue mentioned it, Alyssa wondered that herself. The entire time that Lord Falgerth had been present, the dark black gemstone had given her the creeps. It had seemed to almost *radiate* evil, and it had felt as though it were watching her, *probing* her, actually trying to see her very insides. It still freaked her out to think about it.

"Do you think that he'll come back?" she asked Blue, hoping that he would say 'No.'

But before the unicorn could answer, another, barely audible and distant sounding voice interrupted them. It sounded like a far off person yelling, their voice carried by the wind.

"Blue," it seemed to be calling, and as a group, they all turned to find a barely visible outline of woman floating in the air about ten feet away. It was the Queen, and she was 'ghosting'.

"I don't have the power to spare for conversation," she continued hurriedly, "so please, don't ask questions, just listen.

"Falgerth has retrieved Leviathan's Jewel from behind the broken Shield. It is an old and very powerful stone, and it is full of Evil. He uses it to magically assail me and my Shielding of you almost constantly. That's why he appeared to you, to see if he would have better luck by Ghosting. I managed to ward off this attack, but I don't know how much longer I can last. If you sense my shielding fail, Blue, at all costs you must magically shield yourself and the children! He has no idea that the girl child is the Ancient One's carrier, and he must not find out! He would destroy her. She, herself, is defenseless against him.

"Blue, Falgerth has turned his army away from Altian, and races them toward Spellcasting Peak. He has also sent messengers to the Harriden, and they have already taken up positions against you. He plans to stop you, and anyone else, from ever reaching the mountain, and your Quest has become that much harder because of it. Your three Silver Sentinels as well as what's left of Andwar are riding like the wind to join you. You must go to Cliffland now, where they will meet you, to appeal to the Clifflanders for help. Your brother has consented to carry Lord Abigale. He also will help you. And he carries my staff into battle.

"My power fades, Blue, but I will do what I can, while I can. I will tell you this one last thing, though, your Quest is the greatest that any Blue Unicorn has ever undertaken! You dare not fail. All Tanzal depends on you!"

And with that, the Queen's Ghost disappeared. Everyone was silent for a moment, thinking about everything that had just happened.

"Well, I'll tell you one thing," Raspal said, breaking the silence. "And that is that no unicorn is 'riding like the wind' if they're carrying Fat Abby. Your brother is probably lucky if he can even walk."

Blue snorted. "Darius can carry him. He is one of the strongest Unicorns ever foaled. And even under such a weight, I am sure that the rest of the herd is still having a hard time keeping up with him. He is, after all, The Third Silver Sentinel! Come, children, lunch is done. You will ride on me for the rest of the day, for safety and speed. Time to mount.

"We ride now for Cliffland! And war!"

The rest of that day was a long, fast ride. They had redistributed the packs between all seven ponies, making them each quite a bit lighter, but they were still hard pressed to keep Blue's pace. He spoke not at all as he ran, and the expression on his face was nothing short of grim. Now and then, Alyssa spotted wolves running alongside them as singles, but more often in large packs. There seemed to be more of them, and she asked Sturgill about it. He said that there were now over a hundred following them. Two more packs had joined up.

They left the Starfire Mountains near noon and began to run across rolling, grass covered plains. Low hills marched along their left side and as evening approached, the trail turned and headed straight for them.

The dark clouds that had been gathering for the last two days now finally broke into a light rain, but Alyssa could tell that it wouldn't be long before it was a full-blown downpour.

"I know of a Warming Cave, Blue," Sturgill yelled into the wind as they ran. "It's just a little ways ahead, and off to the left. We can't run all night. I think we should stop there."

"Lead the way," the unicorn replied. The rain was becoming heavier, and now Alyssa could hear the crashing of distant thunder. Her clothes were quickly getting soaked through and the idea of a dry cave and maybe a fire appealed to her.

A few yards further, the black wolf took a right hand turn and headed down a narrow trail running through a stand of stunted cedar trees. On the other side, they came face to face with an opening that led into a cave in a dirt hillside. Large rocks had been stacked around it in an arch to keep the dirt and mud from sliding down and closing it up, and the weeds in the front had been cleared away in places and trampled flat in others. All in all it had the look of ownership about it. It looked like maybe it was someone's home—or at least someplace they stayed quite a bit.

"Wait here," Sturgill said. "I'll go in and make sure that no one else has taken shelter tonight. Don't want to intrude without asking—or walk into a surprise fight!"

It was only a moment later when Sturgill reappeared.

"It's all right," he said. "Nobody's here. Come on in."

Alyssa and Brett had to dismount Blue in order to enter, and the unicorn had to duck his horn and bend his knees slightly as well. The ponies had no problem fitting and followed without even so much as asking. Apparently, they didn't like standing in the rain either.

Five feet into the cave it opened up into a large cavern. Several homemade log chairs as well as a log bench were circled around a small fireplace in the east wall. Somehow—and Alyssa suspected Blue's magic—a new fire was already ablaze inside it, casting dancing shadows against the rock walls. The fireplace's blackened flue looked like it was made out of some sort of beaten iron and exited the cave wall on an angle directly behind it. Several fist-sized holes had been cut into the same rock wall to allow fresh air as well as light into the cavern. A faint mist from the rain blew in as well.

"You can set the packs over there," Blue said indicating the south wall, which was away from the light breeze. The ponies had already lined themselves up against it, and most had their heads down. Several looked like they were already asleep. Alyssa felt sorry for them as she and Brett lifted off their packs. All of their saddle blankets were drenched in sweat from the day's hard ride, and a couple looked like they'd been rubbed raw in spots by their leather straps. They were definitely some tired ponies.

Suddenly, as she and Brett were lifting off the last pack, Alyssa heard Sturgill behind her growling deep in his throat. It was a terrifying, guttural sound, unlike any growl he'd ever made before— even the one he'd made at Lord Falgerth. It was the sound of a trapped animal, about to fight for its life. It sent a sudden bolt of fear racing down her back, and she whirled to see what he was growling at.

What Alyssa saw almost made her heart stop.

Crawling into the cave on its hands and knees was a huge, green ogre. It was so big that its back scraped the top of the entrance cave as it crawled, and when it did stand up inside, it had to duck its head slightly to avoid hitting the ceiling. Its skin was dry and gnarled and a bright, mint green, with splotches of brown liver spots sprayed across it like malignant freckles, while the hair on its misshapen head and hunched back was dark black, setting the two in sharp contrast. Its eyes glowed fire red as it looked around at the cave's occupants.

This is an Ogre's cave! Alyssa thought suddenly. *Oh, great! We're camping in an Ogre's cave!*

The Ogre took a step forward and clenched both of its large hands into fists. It looked like it was going to attack. Alyssa didn't know if a unicorn—even a Blue one—could handle a creature this massive, but she had feeling that she was just about to find out.

Still growling ferociously, Sturgill launched himself at the green monster's leg, while out of the corner of her eye, Alyssa saw Brett draw his sword and step forward. Blue was also moving forward, his horn down and pointing directly at the Ogre's stomach.

But Sturgill didn't land on the Ogre's leg. Instead, he simply disappeared into the creature's body like Brett had done when he fell down the Gnome Hole. One minute he was there, and the next he wasn't. However, Alyssa could still hear him growling just as plain as day. But now he sounded as if he were behind the Ogre.

And then, a sudden bolt of what looked like blue lightening flew from the unicorn's horn, striking the Ogre directly in the chest.

In a brilliant flash of light, the huge green beast exploded into a whirlwind of sparkling black, blue and green magic lights. They spun all about the cavern like a swarm of ghostly silent, glittering bees.

Then, as swiftly as they had come, they abruptly disappeared, leaving behind a completely bewildered black wolf. Sturgill was still growling as he glared around himself, trying to figure out where the ogre had disappeared to.

"It was a shadow, Sturgill," Blue said. "Just an image thrown at us from afar by Lord Falgerth. But once again, it was a very real-looking casting."

"He's tricked me twice in one day," Sturgill muttered with a tone of self-disgust. "I've never seen anything that true-to-life, even in 'Casting Contests' at the Fair. He has become very powerful indeed."

Blue nodded his head grimly. "Yes," he said. "With one hand, he slowly wears down the Queen and the remaining three Mages of the Wizarding Council, and with the other, he harasses me with ghosts and shadows so real-looking that I've never seen their equal. I imagine that he may very well cast shadows at me for most of the night. He apparently has power to spare, and he intends to wear me down as well."

Blue walked over to the cave entrance and looked out into the growing dark and pounding rain. High in the clouds, lightening flashed, illuminating the skeletal fingers of a distant dead tree. The unicorn glanced back at Alyssa and Brett.

"It's time for you to sleep," he said. "We have a long couple of days ahead of us before we reach Cliffland. I'm going to stand guard just outside the cave, where any 'cast shadows' he throws won't bother you. Sturgill will guard the inside, along with Raspal when he returns. Do try to sleep, and remember that shadows can never hurt you."

And with that Blue turned and strode out into the night. Alyssa had intended to object and tell him that they didn't mind and wouldn't be scared, but he was gone too fast. She hated to see him having to spend the night out standing in a downpour, but what could she do? Maybe he didn't really mind it; Katie's horses back home didn't seem to anyways. They always simply lined up side by side, turned their butts to the storm and stood there through the night. And in the morning, they ran around and bucked and kicked the same as always—maybe even more so.

Brett and Alyssa arranged their sleeping quilts near the dying fire and then snuggled deep down into them. As the flames died slowly down, the lightening when it flashed more brightly lit the cave. Thunder always followed, sometimes distant and faint, but more often near and crashing.

Oftentimes, though, the lightening that lit the cave's walls was blue instead of white, and no thunder followed. Each time, Alyssa knew, another shadow had been destroyed.

CHAPTER TEN

Councils of War

Alyssa woke the next morning to find beams of sunlight shining through the air holes in the cave's wall behind the fireplace. She glanced around and saw that Brett and her were alone with Sturgill and the packs. At some point in the night, the ponies must have left. The unicorn also was nowhere to be seen.

Sitting up, she stretched her arms, while Brett stirred at her side. The black wolf lifted his head from his paws and yawned widely. He then licked himself on his forelegs.

"Where did everyone go?" she asked.

"They're out grazing," Sturgill replied. "The rain lifted around midnight, and they left a short while after that. Raspal still hasn't come back. I'm not sure where he is—he is after all a fox—but I'm sure that he plans on catching up with us sometime today."

Alyssa nudged Brett with her foot and said, "Time to get up," then walked over to the packs and pulled out a breakfast of biscuits and fruit. She also took out some more jerky for the wolf, but hesitated to give it to him. Sturgill just laughed at her, and then came over and took the deer jerky from her hand.

"Still worried about me and my pack, I see," he said with a chuckle. "Well, don't be, Alyssa. I'm too old to care about appearances. I know who and what I am, and I'm very happy with it. Anyways, I've walked too many of the far and wild places to ever be tamed. You can feed me all the man-food you want; it won't change me into something that I'll never be."

Brett came over and helped himself to some breakfast as well. He didn't say anything and he seemed like he was still half asleep and grumpy. Typical Brett, Alyssa thought.

After they finished, she and Brett cleaned up and then went outside. A brisk wind had blown the sky free of clouds and the day was bright and sunny. A fresh, after-the-rain smell filled the air, and here and there, bare patches of wet earth steamed in the early morning sunshine. In a nearby clearing, Alyssa spied the unicorn and all the ponies. Blue glanced up at her and then whinnied. The entire herd quit grazing and trotted over.

"I'm glad to see you awake," he said. "I let you sleep in because we've got a long ride ahead of us, and both you and the ponies needed the rest, but it *is* time to be going."

"Are we gonna be riding all day again?" Alyssa asked. She tried to keep her voice sounding neutral, but was afraid that she failed. She was getting very saddle sore and having a hard time hiding it.

"More like two-and-a-half days," Blue replied. "But you'll be riding me the entire way, for speed, so it shouldn't be that bad. We really have no choice. Cliffland borders the Impassable Mountains—it's actually on our way. In the old times it was Tanzal's first line of defense against the Black Lands. The Ancient One himself was born a Clifflander."

"Do you think they'll help us?" Brett asked. "I mean do they have an alliance with you, or something?"

Blue thought about this for a moment. "No, not formally, I guess. But the Wizarding Council and Castle Altian have always been able to count on the Clifflanders. They are the ancient enemies of the Harriden, and I *know* that the Harriden are helping Lord Falgerth. If there is anything truly evil in all of Tanzal, it is the people and the land of Harriden. Their country was cut in half by the creation of the Northern Shield, and they have always resented it—as well as the diminishing of their dark powers that it caused. But they've never been able to do much about it—until now that is."

Great, Alyssa thought, *more enemies bent on my destruction! And now it sounds like it's an entire country – and its army!*

"Anyway," Blue finished. "It's time to be going. Let's pack up."

* * *

For the next two days the group climbed higher and higher through rough, broken hills. They marched their way along thin, rocky trails in the bottom of ravines and creek beds, as well as wide, dusty ones along the ridge tops. The air as well as the trees thinned as they went, and the mornings were cool and breezy—almost to the point of frost. Up here, summer was on its last hurrah, and the smell of autumn was thick in the air. Even an occasional, overly anxious leaf was already starting to turn red or yellow.

The third morning dawned clear and cold, and the small lake that they had camped next to had a thin layer of ice around its edges, crawling out in places toward the center for as far as a foot. The ponies were quick to break it with their hooves to get their morning drink.

"From now on, Sturgill," Blue said as they packed up for the day's ride. "No more wolves. They'd just cause trouble with the Clifflanders and their sheep. Only you and Raspal should come into the valley with us. Have the others go around and wait for us on the valley's far side."

Sturgill sat on his haunches and howled long and deep. It was returned by a chorus of barks, yips and howls in the hills all around them, some very close and some so distant that they could only faintly be heard. Alyssa hadn't seen a single wolf, other than Sturgill, since they'd entered these mountains, but apparently they were still here.

"How much farther is it to Cliffland?" she asked Blue with a hopeful tone.

"About two hours, or so," he answered. "But probably a little less. We could have made it last night, but I wanted to arrive in the daylight. The Clifflander's don't like night arrivals, even if they are expecting you."

For the first hour that morning, the trail rose steeply, winding its way through thin stands of pines and aspens. It was rocky and tight and the herd climbed it in single file, with Raspal bringing up the rear. The fox had slipped quietly back into camp yesterday morning and hadn't said much since, which was unusual for him. Blue had quizzed him about where he'd been, but he'd simply muttered something about being "out scouting" and clammed up. The unicorn hadn't pushed the issue. What Raspal was up to was the very least of his worries.

As the group neared the top of the trail, it gradually leveled out, and Alyssa could now see that this was in fact a high mountain pass. Judging by the continuous line of peaks rising on either side of her and marching off into the distance toward both horizons, she figured that it was the only one for miles around. The air was now very thin and cold, and a stiff breeze blew over the ridgeline.

When Alyssa and Brett finally topped the ridge, the sight that met their eyes took their breath away.

About three thousand feet directly below them lay a large green valley. It was only about a three or four miles wide but stretched away to their right and left for as far as the eye could see. The valley floor was cut into perfect squares that looked from here to be about a mile wide and a mile deep. Some were bright green, the color of a newly mowed lawn, while others were a pale yellow, like ripened grain. Still others were quite obviously large stands of trees—fruit trees, Alyssa supposed, apples, peaches, and apricots, that sort of stuff.

But the perfectly groomed farmland wasn't what caught Alyssa and Brett's instant attention and awe.

It was the mountains on the other side of this valley. They were taller and more sheer than any she had ever seen—and she had been all over the Sierra Nevada and Rocky Mountains with her dad while climbing and camping. These were incredibly, impossibly, mind-bendingly high, with one sheer cliff stacked on top of another until they reached far into the sky above her. They were made of a brownish, red rock, which was lined with a thin layer of grey about every thousand feet or so, while the topmost segment was composed of a dark black, glassy stone, like obsidian, that jutted sharply up into freestanding pinnacles and spires. The upper layer made it look like the cliffs were wearing a crazy, mangled black crown.

It took almost a full minute before Alyssa's mind would accept that what she was seeing was actually real and not an illusion—although here in Tanzal, she was learning not to trust even her own eyes. She had seen El Capitan once in Yosemite National Park, and knew that it was about two thousand feet straight up; these mountains were easily four times as high—and just as vertical! It was like Zion's National Park near the Narrows, only ten times as big.

When she realized that she was holding her breath, Alyssa let it out in a rush. Her dad would freak if he ever saw this! This was a sheer cliff that ran for as far as she could see in both directions and was over eight thousand feet high!

Brett whistled lowly in amazement. "Now *that's* a Big Wall!" he breathed. "Man, I'd like to climb that someday."

"No one and nothing could climb those mountains," Blue stated in a matter-of-fact voice. "Even with magic, it couldn't be done. The Clifflanders are accomplished cliff-climbers—the best in all Tanzal—but they are the ones who named them. They call them The Impassable Mountains for good reason. Look, down in Cliffland, my brother comes!"

Both Brett and Alyssa turned and stared down. Running across the green fields below was a group of dots, at least fifty or more, Alyssa estimated, but it was hard to count from way up here. They looked like a herd of wild horses, racing the wind, but they weren't, she knew.

They were unicorns. An entire herd of them.

Out in front, three of the dots were pulling away—three dots that were different from all the rest. These dots were pure white, the color of newly fallen snow, and every few seconds or so they would glint and glimmer, like a diamond turning in bright light. They were the Silver Sentinels, Alyssa knew, and just seeing them run free made her heart soar! A feeling of lightness and absolute freedom washed over her! She suddenly wanted to run herself.

"Andwar will be reformed!" Blue cried out. "It will ride again! Hold on tight, children! Now you shall see a unicorn's true speed. Let those who fall behind catch up as they can. *The time to run has come!*"

What happened next was more of a blur for Alyssa than anything she had yet experienced in Tanzal, or her entire life for that matter! For an instant, they were frozen in time and space, like when you reach the top of the first hill of a very tall roller coaster, and then Blue jumped forward, racing down the mountain in a sudden rush. Down, down, and down they went, the wind roaring by them. Rocks, trees and small hills soared past in a blinding blur. It was just like a rushing roller coaster—only it was one that always went down, never up, and kept picking up speed as it flew.

How the unicorn kept his footing was beyond Alyssa. She couldn't see the ground, much less make out where the trail was or the rocks that covered it. She could, however, see sparks flying from Blue's hooves as he ran across the stones below, so many sparks in fact that they almost looked like flames. Magic, Alyssa figured. Unicorn Magic.

In no time at all, they were down on the valley floor, racing across its first green field. Ahead, Alyssa could see a medium sized river approaching rapidly, and for an instant she wondered how they were going to cross it. Her question was answered a moment later when they arrived.

Without missing a single stride, Blue jumped, launching himself through the air. It was at least twenty-five feet from bank to bank, and the unicorn made it effortlessly. He landed on the other side as smoothly as an Olympic ski jumper gently touching down on frozen snow. Alyssa didn't even feel them land, but found herself once again racing forward. The river now rapidly receded behind them even as three white shapes raced toward them, growing suddenly in size like magic.

Blue and his Silver Sentinels met in a melee of sound and fury. While the three white unicorns raced around him in a circle, bucking, neighing and throwing their heads and manes, Blue reared up three times and pawed the air with flashing hooves. Each time he rose, Alyssa felt as if she were going to fall off. She twisted her hands tightly in his mane, while Brett wrapped his arms around her waist.

Then, like a wave of rolling thunder, they were surrounded by the rest of the herd and engulfed by the deafening pounding of two hundred hooves on fifty thundering unicorns as they raced around and around. Dust, flying grass and a variety of colored magic-lights filled the air.

And then, as fast as it had started, it suddenly stopped, and all the unicorns stood stock-still. They formed a circle around Blue and stared intently in at him, their horns held high, their breathing heavy. The largest of the three white unicorns now stepped forward and dipped his pure silver horn. Alyssa caught her breath at his shear size. He was as tall as, if not taller than, the Belgian draw horses she saw pulling horse carts during Christmas in downtown Salt Lake City. His build, however, was nothing like a drawhorse's. He was sleek and limber, and under his snow-white coat, his muscles stood out like a well-conditioned racehorse's. An aura of pure strength and confidence radiated from him.

"The Unicorn's Quest has begun," Blue stated loudly and solemnly. He stared directly at his older brother when he spoke and both his eyes and his voice were hard and grim. "It began with the destruction of The Northern Shield just a few miles from here. It continued with the running battles against with Lord Falgerth's army that has seen many of Andwar fall, and it will be finished only when we have helped rebuild the Ancient One's Shield. All that is needed of his magic has come to us, and I shall see it taken to the Kolvard's Steps, or die trying. Only those who truly wish it should ride with me to the finish, though we may be riding to our doom, and the end of Andwar."

There was moment of silence among the herd and then Darius, the Third Silver Sentinel, threw back his head and laughed out loud. His eyes sparkled with pure amusement.

"Who is this stern warrior that stands before us?" the white unicorn cried out in mirth. "And what has he done with my quiet and thoughtful brother? Surely, this can't be him?" Darius laughed again and then gazed hard at Blue. His eyes became soft, and a tear glistened in the corner of one.

"Father always said that you would rise to your quest," he continued quietly. "He would be bursting with pride for you if he were here right now. You have brought great honor to our family."

Suddenly, Darius wheeled. He threw his head and neighed loudly. His horn shone like a silver beacon.

"My father died valiantly in battle!" he cried out to the herd. "Two Black Trolls went down before him. He was Chief of Andwar, and the Keeper of the Secret Flame. I hereby abdicate my right as oldest son to take his place and ask that you confirm my brother, the Blue Unicorn, in my stead. It is time for a new Chief of Andwar! The Flame has been dimmed for far too long! Let us choose now, rekindle the Flame, and ride together to Our Quest's end. Let Lord Falgerth again feel our power and tremble before it!"

As one, the entire herd reared up before Blue and neighed loudly. The sound was deafening, and both Brett and Alyssa covered their ears. When they came down, their hooves struck the earth like the rumbling of a hundred earthquakes. It was exactly the same as when Blue struck the ground with his hooves, only fifty times louder. It was an avalanche of sound. The herd now thronged forward, pressing in from all around. Their heads were lowered and their horns held level until all of them were touching either Blue's horn itself or another horn that touched his.

It was nothing short of amazing to Alyssa that one horn or another didn't instantly skewer her, but, in fact, she wasn't even touched.

What happened next was something that Alyssa would never forget no matter how long she lived. Not a single word was spoken, but when all the horns were touching, a light crackling sound began, like electricity over high-voltage power lines. A moment later, multicolored sparks and flashes ran around, across and even through the horns themselves. The sound quickly rose in pitch and volume, and the electrical charges raced around and around in increasing frenzy. Rainbow colored, heatless flames now flew out in all directions, and every hair on Alyssa's body stood on end. She looked down to find that she was entirely covered with the incandescent glow of static electricity.

Saint Elmo's Fire! she thought to herself. This was the same thing that sailors saw during electrical storms out on the ocean!

But she only had a second to marvel at it because at that moment the air was shattered by a huge clap of thunder as a bolt of lightening fell out of the clear blue sky. It struck directly on the top of Blue's silver horn.

As one, the unicorns threw themselves backward, leaving Blue alone. He now stood completely motionless, like a stone statue of a unicorn, and his erect horn glowed with a bright orange fire, the color of molten steel. For a moment, Alyssa thought that she could see the outline of a tall flame rising above him, but then it was gone. The glow of Blue's horn slowly faded and he dipped it down in submission to those around him.

"I accept the honor," he said quietly. "Andwar will ride at least one more time, with me as Chief. But come, our time grows short, and the Councils of War await us!"

With that, Blue trotted forward, and the herd parted to let him through. His brother and the other two Silver Sentinels fell in behind him as he passed. The rest of the herd silently followed suit. Once he was in the clear, Blue broke into a ground-covering lope.

"You have just witnessed something that only happens once in a generation," he said quietly to Alyssa and Brett over his shoulder. "And you are the only humans that I've ever heard of that were within the circle during The Choosing. I didn't plan this, and I'm not sure, but I think you may now be a part of Andwar. I will test you later, when we have more time."

It wasn't long before Alyssa could see a village in the distance. It was nestled against the cliff wall on the valley's far side and was surrounded by hundreds of tall cottonwood trees. As they approached, she could make out the houses on the outskirts of town. They were square and squat, with some of them more than thirty feet long and twenty feet wide, but none of more than ten feet tall. All of the houses had low, pitched roofs made of thatched rushes and each had at least one chimney, and many of the larger ones had two. Both the house's walls and their chimneystacks were made of hand-chiseled and closely-fitted red rock—which was the exact same color as the stone in the cliffs. Alyssa figured that they probably quarried it somewhere nearby.

Blue slowed his pace to a trot as they reached the first of the homes, and several people came out of their doors to see the spectacle of fifty unicorns running through the street. But they didn't watch the herd for long; almost immediately they stared in open amazement at Alyssa and Brett as they passed. Alyssa glanced down at herself to see what they were staring at. She was dressed in a t-shirt, Levi's jeans and her cross-country running shoes. Normal enough—at least to her and Brett—but to the Clifflanders they probably looked like spacesuits.

Great, she thought, *I've finally found actual people to talk to, and they think we're freaks!*

The Clifflanders themselves were dressed in loose-fitting pants and long dresses made of a light brown or olive green fabric. All the grown men Alyssa saw, and quite a few of the boys, carried bows strapped across their backs with at least one but sometimes two full quivers of arrows. Many also carried large swords in thick leather scabbards on their waists. Some wore light mail or leather jerkins. Most of them nodded or waved to Blue as he passed, and Blue tipped his horn in return.

"They are geared for war," he said quietly as he walked. "My guess is that Lord Abigale has been busy."

As they went, the houses grew bigger and closer together. Several were now two stories high, and many were shops instead of houses. Their open windows displayed the wares of their keepers. One was a bakery and another a butcher's shop. Several were clothiers, and a small one on a side street looked like a shoemaker's store.

Near the end of the street, they came upon the largest, two-story building that they had seen yet. It was easily sixty feet long and forty feet wide, and it was made of an entirely different rock. This, Alyssa figured as she looked closely at it, was marble—a glassy white marble streaked with bands of black and rose. Many of the marble blocks were carved in bas-relief with figures of fauns and nymphs dancing in woodlands and mountains. They were incredibly detailed, and some, at the corner of her eyes, even seemed to be moving.

In front of the building was seated a very large man, and as Blue approached, he pulled himself slowly to his feet. He wore a long, flowing white robe that hid most of his shape, but Alyssa was sure that he was pushing a good three hundred and fifty pounds. He was mostly bald, with just a few long white hairs hanging from the back his white scalp, and he used a tall, gnarled staff for support.

The staff had a very large, deep green Tanzalite stone embedded in its top.

"Greetings, Lord Abigale," Blue said with a nod. "I see that you've been busy."

"No," he replied, shaking his head in resignation. "I have not. I arrived here myself only late last night. The Clifflanders were gearing for war long before me. They blame the Harriden for the destruction of the shield. They mean to strike before they become too strong with Black Magic."

"Will they meet with me first? We are on the same mission."

"They're waiting for you inside," Abigale replied. "I'm sorry. I know that you would like to rest, but our time is short. I am in constant contact with the Queen, and both our shielding powers are dwindling, even with the aid of our stones. We have only a few days left. Come, I have told them of your Quest, and they wish to know your needs."

Blue nodded. "Climb down, children," he said. "I would have you follow me on your feet. Darius, you also will accompany me. The rest of you may return to the fields to graze. Tomorrow will be a long day."

As Alyssa scrambled down off of Blue's back, Lord Abigale stepped over and touched her shoulder. For a moment, his eyes went distant and clouded, and she had a strange feeling that she was being probed, then he suddenly pulled his hand away. His eyes quickly refocused, and he gazed down at her with a mixture of sudden surprise and awe.

"I've studied the Ancient One's magic all my life," he said quietly. "It's been my private obsession. I sense that *all* of his great magic now resides inside you. How you came by it, I do not know, but I did know that I would find it there. What I didn't expect to find is a huge, natural magic that is all your own, a different kind of magic that I've never felt before, from your own world."

He paused for a minute, shaking his head in wonder. "As far as I can tell with such a short probing, your own inborn magic is as great if not greater than his. How one person can hold so much magic is beyond me. It's incredible. It's almost like you're Tanzalite, made flesh and come to life. If only you were trained, what a weapon you would be!"

Still shaking his head, Lord Abigale turned to lead the way inside. Sturgill and Raspal, who had trailed the herd into town, now slipped up next to Alyssa and Brett.

"I doubt that the Clifflanders would wish a wolf to come to counsel," Lord Abigale remarked, glancing down. He held open the building's heavy wooden doors so that Blue and Darius could walk through. Both had to duck their heads and horns and Darius' hindquarters almost brushed the top of the doorjamb. "Perhaps you should wait outside, Sturgill. You as well, Raspal."

"If they don't wish my presence," the black wolf answered softly. "Then they can attempt to kill me. Otherwise, I will stay at the girl-child's side."

"Suit yourself, Pack Leader. I was only making a suggestion."

Raspal didn't say a word, but simply followed on Sturgill's heels.

Inside they passed single file down a narrow hallway. At the end, Blue came up against another heavy wooden door which he pushed open with his head. The room they entered was open and airy. It was a thirty-foot by thirty-foot 'Great Room' with a vaulted ceiling that rose all the way to the roof's exposed rough pine beams twenty feet above. The ceiling itself was made of darkly stained, tongue and groove pine, and all around the room on the second floor were a series of balconies filled with chairs. It looked like enough seating for at least a hundred people.

For a moment, Alyssa was struck with the impression that it was a miniature Roman Amphitheater, but that feeling quickly passed. It was more likely a council room for government, or a theatre—or maybe even both.

In the center of this room stood a large wooden table with a group of ten men standing around it. They were dressed much the same as the rest of the men in town, and all but one of them carried large, heavy-handled broad blades on their hips and wore coats of thick, ringed mail that hung down to their waists. The only warrior without a sword had a tall longbow strapped down his back. It's curved bow reached from his calves to a foot above his head, and he carried two full quivers of arrows as well.

Together as one, they looked up and watched as Blue and his strange entourage entered. Most of them scowled openly at the sight of both the wolf and the fox.

"Greetings, Unicorn," one of the taller men said with a nod toward Blue. His voice was deep and his tone somber. "We're glad to see that you're safely here, and we eagerly anticipate a Blue Unicorn's aid and counsel. But I must say that we're not as excited to see the Sheepkiller that accompanies you."

Sturgill stepped forward and stared unwaveringly at the large man.

"I have never killed a sheep in my entire life," he said in a quiet but firm voice. "Nor has any Talking Wolf that I know of. In fact, my pack and I have fought and killed many wild wolves and Lycants on the borders of Cliffland that do. I have probably saved more of your sheep from death than even your best sheepherder, and I will not tolerate your saying otherwise."

For a moment, the room was filled with an uncomfortable silence. Several of the men shifted back and forth on their feet, and a few stared nervously at both Blue and Darius. Alyssa could tell that fighting a Unicorn was the last thing they wanted to do.

"My apologies, Master Wolf," the man finally answered with a faint smile. "You are well-spoken and brave, and I believe you to be honest. I welcome both you and your pack's aid. Please take no offense. Black times test patience and nerves."

"Your apology is accepted," Sturgill answered graciously. "And no offense taken. I save my offense for our mutual enemy."

The tall man now glanced at Raspal, who was casually sitting on his haunches next to Brett, his tail wrapped around his feet.

"And I suppose that you don't kill chickens, either," he said.

"Well," Raspal drawled in amusement. "Not any of *yours.*" He then paused and glanced off, as if in deep thought, then looked back and finished, "At least not *lately,* anyways."

With a chuckle, the red fox lifted a paw, licked it and began to calmly clean his face.

Most of the warriors broke a smile at this, and several laughed out loud and shook their heads in wonder at his insolence. Only one on the far side of the table scowled. He was a good foot shorter than the rest, and very stocky, almost dwarfish-looking, Alyssa thought.

"That's the best you can expect from a fox," Blue interjected. "He is the Queen's own confidant, and emissary. I personally vouch for him. He is my friend."

"Then that's good enough for me," the man said. "We have never met before, Master Unicorn, so let me introduce myself and my Generals. I am Kandal, King of Cliffland, and this is Goslin, the Captain of my swordsmen, and Burrow, the Captain of my Archers." He indicated first the short, still scowling warrior and then the tall, longhaired bowman who stood next to him. They both nodded at the unicorn.

"I am pleased to meet you," Blue replied. "I have heard a great deal about you, and Cliffland is lucky to have such a King. I am Blue, The Blue Unicorn and Chief of Andwar, and this is Sturgill, leader of the Talking Wolves; Raspal, the Queen's emissary; and Alyssa and Brett Turner, who are visiting Tanzal. Of course, you have already met my brother Darius and Lord Abigale."

"So Andwar has re-chosen its Chief, have they?" the King mused. "This is welcome news, and I congratulate you. But come, let me show you the situation we have and ask your advice."

He waved them toward the table, and Alyssa now saw that they had maps and diagrams laid out across it. Blue, Sturgill and Darius all stepped forward quickly with interest, and Lord Abigale waddled up right behind them. Alyssa and Brett held back, not knowing if he'd meant them as well, and Raspal showed no interest whatsoever in anything except the cleaning of his face.

"Lord Falgerth is encamped with the Harriden army at the start of the Impassable Mountains," King Kandal said, pointing at a spot on the map. "My spies tell me that they are now well dug in, and still digging. For reasons that I'm told have to do with your quest, they have surrounded the base of Spellcasting Mountain and cut off all of the approaches to Kolvard's steps."

"Not all," one of the General's objected. It was the warrior with the bow strapped to his back.

"All that a Unicorn could take," Kandal replied, glancing over at him.

The man nodded in agreement. "True enough. Even with magic, unicorns can't climb cliffs."

King Kandal turned to face Blue. "So I guess what I need to know is: Where do you need to go to rebuild the shield, and what do you need with you? What's it going to take? And what can we do to help? It goes without saying that if you do rebuild the shield, the Harriden army's magical strength will be cut in half, at the very least. Their witches have grown very strong since it fell. We have done nothing to them in over a hundred years, and yet now they throw curses at us daily."

"Most of our lambs in the last month have been stillborn," Goslin said. His voice was hard and angry. "Some are born with two heads, and others with none! We *will* put an end to this."

"The girl-child will ride on me," Blue said. "And together we must make it to Kolvard's steps. That is all I require from you. The boy shall ride Darius and fight beside you."

"I must object, My Liege!" Goslin exclaimed. "It is one thing to ally ourselves with Talking Wolves—they can fight their own kind, and those horrid Lycants—but it is quite another to allow *children* to ride to war! Why not bring the women as well!"

"You have a valid point, Goslin. What say you, Chief Unicorn? Surely it would be safer to leave the children here in town."

Blue nodded solemnly. "I understand your concern, but let me tell you; the Ancient One—the Wizard known in Cliffland as Kolvard, the Old—has somehow cast a spell through time on the girl-child. She contains all his ancient power, and has found his lost, Fourth Book of Magic. Truly, only she needs to go to Kolvard's Steps with his book. I am but a strong ride. The boy now," and at this, Blue glanced back and smiled at Brett, "He can take care of himself just fine. He can stand toe-to-toe with any warrior of Harriden—or even three or four."

Several of the men chuckled at this, and shook their heads in amusement. Goslin stepped forward, his hands on his hips, his eyes challenging.

"I don't mean to question your judgment, Chief Unicorn, but that is a true wonder that I must see with my own eyes. I am more to his size than any other here; perhaps we should fence a bit? Nothing serious, just a small demonstration of his skill."

"No," Blue answered firmly. "You must take my word, it would be dangerous for you. Even I don't dare fence with him."

At this, several of the men burst out in full laughter. But the king shook his head and scowled lightly.

"Goslin makes a good point," he said. "And I can't see the harm in light swordplay. I, too, am intrigued by this and would like to see his skills."

Approval from the King was all that Goslin needed. He pulled his large broadsword free and stepped away from the table toward the center of the room.

"I'm a grown man, and I'm willing to take this risk," he said with a sardonic chuckle. "Come, boy, let's see what you can do!"

"I still object," Blue said. "You can ill afford to lose a man, much less a Captain, on the eve of battle!"

"Oh, let them fight!" Raspal suddenly spoke up. He stopped cleaning his face and stared with irritation at the King and his men.

"It'll teach the arrogant ass a lesson. But I warn you, Captain of the Swordsmen, I won't endanger *my tail* a second time!"

Blue glanced at the faces all around him and saw what Alyssa could also plainly see: At this point, they weren't going to take no for an answer. Their curiosity was too high.

"Fine," he said. "Go ahead, Brett. But remember, Kandal, I objected strongly to this."

"Your objections have been noted," the King replied. "And Goslin's decision is all his own."

With a nod from Blue, Brett pulled out the Sword of Cabral and stepped over to the center of the room. The King and his generals quickly formed a loose circle around the combatants. Most of their faces were smiling and laughing. Apparently, this was going to be fun to watch. Only Burrow seemed to pay attention to Brett's sword. His eyes narrowed quickly when he saw it, and its large Tanzalite gemstone, and then he shook his head in amusement and wonder.

"Don't worry, son," Goslin said as he made his first thrust. "I'll be gentle."

Almost the instant their swords crossed, Brett's eyes glazed over and a faint, distant smile touched the corner of his lips.

The Sword of Cabral easily parried Goslin' first thrust, then his second, and then a series of rapid cuts. The sword then suddenly took the offensive and quickly struck high, then low, and then in a wide sweep. Goslin himself parried the blows easily, and then, with a low growl, attacked in earnest, his blade moving faster and faster.

The clanging of steel on steel filled the room as Brett and the warrior dueled. Alyssa could see looks of grudging admiration growing on the faces around her.

Suddenly, the sword parried a thrust by Goslin and slipped behind his guard to his shoulder. It sliced as easily through his steel mail coat as a hot knife through butter. Several chain links fell free, clinking on the stone floor.

Goslin stared in wonder at his damaged coat, and then with a loud, frustrated growl, he leapt forward and furiously attacked. His strokes were no longer friendly or gentle at all. They were wide and fast and hard, almost as if he meant to beat Brett by shear weight and force. But the Sword of Cabral had no problem catching and holding every one of them. It moved quickly and easily—almost daintily, Alyssa thought—and only a moment later, it slipped in and cut the mail coat on Goslin's other shoulder.

More chain links fell to the floor.

There were several gasps of wonder. One time was luck; twice was skill. And how could the boy cut through hardened steel so easily? It was almost like he was slitting paper!

Now, Goslin went completely wild. He struck first left, then right, and then, using his all his size and strength, he swung his broadsword high over his head and brought it crashing down directly toward Brett's exposed skull.

This was a battle blow. And everyone there could see it.

Brett's sword quickly crossed sideways above him, catching the large broadsword. They came together with a loud ringing, blade on blade, steel on steel.

And Goslin's sword exploded in his hands.

It shattered into a shower of steel shards.

Alyssa couldn't tell if it was from the sheer force of his swing, or from the Sword of Cabral's magic, but either way, Goslin now found himself holding only a broken hilt of a broadsword and the tip of Brett's blade gently touching his throat.

"Give me another sword!" he growled.

"No," King Kandal stated loudly and firmly. "You have been beaten, fair and square. If this had been battle, you'd now be dead. The boy has proven his worth. He rides with us in the morning."

"Perhaps," Burrow said. "If the boy is going to ride a Silver Unicorn and fight with that blade, he should lead the charge! Oh, don't act so put out, Goslin, you weren't beaten at swordplay; you were beaten with magic! Look closely at that sword—it's the Gnome King's enchanted blade, you fool! You're lucky that you still draw breath. Most who face that sword don't live to talk about it. The unicorn was right—you should never have fought. It was far too dangerous for you."

The king stared intently down at the Sword of Cabral, then smiled ruefully and turned to Blue.

"I guess I have learned a lesson as well," he said. "I won't question your judgment again. But please, tell me what you think we can do for you? As well as the Harriden are dug in behind their spiked pits and moats of oil, I'm afraid that your magic and speed will be of little use. Only with a protracted siege are we going to be able to force our way through. It may take weeks."

"And that is time that we don't have," Lord Abigale said. "Falgerth believes that the Unicorn possesses the magic, and because we shield her, he knows nothing of the girl. But our shielding will last only a few days longer, and then he will quickly discern the truth. When he does, all will be lost. She knows nothing of magic and is defenseless against him. Our battle plans must be fast moving. She needs to reach Kolvard's Steps in the next two days."

"Then I will carry her," Burrow suddenly said. He stepped over to Alyssa and looked her up and down. "She can't weigh more than five stones, six at the most. If it's true that only she needs to go, then she can hike for the most part, and I'll pack her across the Two Faces. I've packed almost as heavy before. And if The Razor terrifies her, she can close her eyes and I will carry her for that as well."

The king and all his men stared down at Alyssa in sudden, thoughtful silence. Some appeared skeptical, but several nodded in agreement.

"Two could go," one of the warriors added. "And each could carry for one face. I would be more than happy to go and take a turn. I have packed heavier!"

Alyssa was just about to ask what they were talking about when Blue did it for her.

"Please, tell me," he said. "What is this discussion about?"

"Leatham's passage," Kandal answered. "It is another way to Kolvard's Steps—a secret trail that only the Clifflanders know about. Every Clifflander boy must take it before he can walk as a warrior. It is a treacherous path through the three peaks just before Spellcasting Mountain that we call the Three Princesses. In places, you must climb up sheer cliffs, and in the end, walk Leatham's Razor over to Spellcasting Peak. Our boys must conquer their fear and climb it, otherwise they can stay with the women and children and make bread and tend to the fires when the men go to work or war."

"And if they fall to their deaths while doing this," Abigale added sarcastically, "then at least they were brave!"

"No one *falls to their deaths*," Burrow replied, a little irritated. "The path has been traveled for hundreds of years, and we climb with steel anchors and ropes in case we slip. If a boy falls at any time during his test, he must start again at the very beginning, but he doesn't die."

"Anywhere Alyssa goes," Brett stated loudly. "I'm going with her. Especially if it's rock climbing!"

Burrow nodded in agreement. "I understand, and I think that it's a good idea. Your sword and my bow together should protect us against anything we encounter on the path. A second warrior could carry you across the two faces, and the third follow in the rear and anchor us."

"No," Brett replied. "You don't get it, do you? If I go, I'm climbing. Nobody's gonna be carrying me anywhere or up anything! I can climb any mountain that you can climb, and if I had all my equipment here, I could probably climb things that you've only dreamed about! And guess what? Alyssa climbs better than me!"

"No I don't," Alyssa objected. Everyone was now staring at her and it made her want to crawl into a corner and hide. "You've been a better climber for a while now. Even Dad thinks so. Last time we went to Arches, he couldn't shut up about your leading out. He says that your only problem is that you need to slow down, or you're gonna have safety issues."

"So you *can* climb cliffs?" Burrow asked Alyssa in wonderment. "You've climbed them before?"

"Yes. I can. I've been hiking since I can remember and my Dad started me climbing by doing Rock Walls at the mall in Second Grade. Brett's been climbing since First. We go camping and do climbs in Cottonwood Canyon or down at Arches almost every weekend. It's my dad's passion. But I think Brett's bragging really badly when he says that he can climb anything that you can. He's still young and much smaller than you. I am too. We wouldn't have your endurance in a long, steep climb, and if the holds are too far apart, we wouldn't be able to follow you.

"But if it's a short climb, with good holds, we could do it. No problem."

"I'll bet I can climb anything that he can climb," Brett restated. "I'd bet money!"

Right then, there was a loud clattering. Alyssa turned to see that Goslin had thrown his broken sword-hilt onto the table among the maps and plans.

"I'm inclined to believe the boy, myself," he said with a rueful smile. "I say, let him climb."

"I agree," the King stated. "What do you say, Chief Unicorn?"

"I don't like the idea of leaving the children," Blue replied. "I've come with them this far; I'd like to see them all the way to the end. And how can you be sure that this pass is not also guarded? I don't say no, but I have reservations."

"Our scouts are using Leatham's Passage to get above Falgerth and spy out him and his army's preparations," Burrow answered. "That's how we know so much. Trust me, this will be much safer for the children than trying to ride your way pell-mell through a raging battle. Anyway, you said it yourself, Falgerth wants you, not the children. The passage will take me six hours at the most. You could easily march and marshal in front of him for that long, and by the time he figures out what's happened, it will be too late. We'll be on Kolvard's Steps behind him. There might not even need to be a battle!"

"I must agree with the Clifflanders, Blue," Lord Abigale spoke up. "But for a different reason than them. I don't think that it's a coincidence that the carrier of his magic can climb cliffs. Kolvard himself was a Clifflander, and—trust me in this—everything about his spells has a purpose. Climbing this passage might be the trigger for this spell. I can feel it in my guts; the girl needs to take Leatham's

Passage. It's important."

Blue stared at the ground for a moment, as if in indecision. He then glanced up and gazed directly at Alyssa.

"I will abide by your choosing. Both ways pose risks. Let your heart tell you. It knows the way."

Alyssa thought for a moment. For her it really wasn't a very hard decision to make—the hard part was going to be leaving Blue and Sturgill behind. She was tired of riding horses—and even Unicorns, for that matter—and she had absolutely no desire whatsoever to join in a full-fledged battle. Watching Sturgill's pack fight the Lycants had been bad enough.

Also, she was excited at the idea of climbing in this strange land. It would be the first time she'd ever gone up a real cliff without her dad, and he wouldn't be mad at her for it because he wouldn't believe her even if she told him the absolute truth!

Anyway, it actually sounded like a pretty tame climb, and safe enough.

"I'll climb," she stated quietly. "It sounds like the quickest way home from here for me and Brett."

Chapter Eleven

The Three Princesses

Long before sunrise the following morning, Burrow Handley's wife shook Alyssa and Brett awake.

"Time to rise, I'm afraid," she said. She spoke softly but her hands were firm and strong as she pulled their covers off of them. She was a matronly and heavyset woman—big-boned as Brett had said—and she always seemed busy with something. "The cavalry's been forming for the better part of two hours now, and plan to ride soon. You'd best start getting ready. I've a cup of Tareroot tea for each of you. It'll wake you quick enough. Also, I've fresh clothes for you, and climbing shoes. Burrow wants you changed because dressed as you are, you stand out like Old Gnomes at a Wood Dance! You can put your dirty clothes in your pack, and carry them if you wish, though I've no idea why a body would wear such outlandish garb!"

Reluctantly, Alyssa pulled herself into a sitting position. She could see that she had little choice. Not only had the blanket been pulled off of her, but it was now in the process of being neatly folded on top of Brett's and packed away into a closet.

After the council had broken up last night, Burrow had taken them back to his house. His wife had cooked them their first hot meal in over two weeks and then made them comfortable in her spare room. Alyssa had slept on a small feather bed—she had never slept on anything so soft in all her life!—while Brett had gladly camped out on a dense rug next to it. Sturgill had slipped into the house on their heels and then quietly curled up at the foot of Alyssa's bed. And although she'd given him several dark glances, Mrs. Handley hadn't said anything out loud. Apparently Burrow had talked to her.

At Blue's urging, they'd gone to bed early yesterday afternoon. Alyssa had no idea what time it was now, but it was still very dark outside the bedroom window. It felt like it was the middle of the night.

Carefully, she sipped the hot liquid from the brown mug that Mrs. Handley had set in front of her, while Brett sipped from his.

"How long before we go?" Brett asked.

"Less than a half-hour, I'd guess," Mrs. Handley replied. "Now finish your tea and get dressed. And be quick about. Burrow is waiting."

The clothes she'd left for them were a set of loose-fitting pants and a tunic, with a belt that held them up. They were a light olive green with shades of brown streaked across them. They looked like Army issued camouflage. *Robin Hood* clothes, as Brett called them. Most of the Archers in town had been wearing much the same style.

The shoes, on the other hand, were different than any they'd seen in town. They were made of a well-tanned, hard black leather, and their soles had been rubbed so extensively with oils that they almost felt like rubber. Alyssa slipped them on and found that they formed to fit her feet perfectly, almost as if they'd been made especially for her. They must have measured her while she was sleeping. She scuffed them against the stone floor; they grabbed and held like there was glue on the bottom.

"These kick butt!" Brett breathed in awe as he scuffed his own shoes against the floor. "They're like spiderman shoes! They stick to everything!"

Out in the kitchen, Mrs. Handley had a small breakfast of scrambled eggs, fried ham and sweet breads set out for them, as well as another cup of Tareroot tea.

"Eat quickly," Burrow said as he sat down next to them and dished himself a plate. "Your horses are saddled and waiting. We won't be riding with the army for long, but I do want to leave with them."

"You mean that we won't be riding Blue or his brother?" Alyssa asked.

"No, it's time for the Blue Unicorn to go on without you. Or is it the other way around? I'm not sure. Either way, your time with him is at its end. I shall take you on the last leg of your journey."

"But I will still accompany you," Sturgill said quietly from his place on the floor beside Alyssa's chair.

"I doubt that you will get far," Burrow replied. "Where we go, only birds and other climbers can follow. Even mountain goats dare not tread these places, or climb these faces."

"Then I will go as far as I can."

Burrow shook his head in irritation. "Suit yourself, Master Wolf."

When they finished with breakfast, Alyssa and Brett went back to their room and packed their old clothes. Hopefully, they would need them again before the day was over. Hopefully, they would soon be back home. Alyssa also carefully wrapped her two virgin Tanzalite stones as well as the Fourth Book of Magic up inside her shirt. The Book was warm to her touch, and it seemed to be humming. It no longer scared her, like it had at first. It was magic, but it was *good* magic, and she was getting used to that. The feel of the Book's warm covers filled her with anticipation. Something was going to happen today. She could sense it. She could feel it deep in her bones. And the Book *knew* it, too. Both of them were ready.

Outside, the sky was full of bright, strange stars, but none of Tanzal's three moons was anywhere to be seen. Most of the houses up and down Burrow's street had lights burning in their windows, and a great many horses and riders were trotting in the pre-dawn dark toward the outskirts of town. Burrow helped them onto a couple of mules that were tied in front of his house, mounting one himself as well. He then took both their mules' reins and led them out into the procession. On her left, Alyssa could see the tall, dark cliff towering above her and blocking out the stars.

She hoped that she wouldn't have to climb anything that was even remotely as tall or sheer as that. There was no way that she could.

"Why are we riding mules?" Brett asked as they went, and Alyssa was glad that he did. She was curious about that herself.

"On the trail we're taking, we will need calm and surefooted animals," Burrow answered. "A mule is calmer by nature and doesn't spook on cliff trails because it can see all four of its feet at the same time. A horse cannot and so may panic."

Alyssa thought about this as the group rode in silence to a large field at the edge of town. She'd never heard it before and so wondered if it was true for mules back on earth as well. Scattered across the grassy meadow in the dark for as far as Alyssa could see were horses and riders, swordsman and bowman, hundreds upon hundreds. Some were saddling or graining their horses, while others stuffed or loaded packs. Most of them, however, stood in groups around small fires, talking and tuning their bows and swords. Their horses stood in straight lines behind them, their heads hung down, packed and ready for war.

Toward the center several large wall tents had been pitched and a bonfire had been built. It was in this direction that Burrow now led Brett and Alyssa's mules.

When they arrived at the fire, Alyssa spied both Blue and his brother, Darius. Blue's other two Silver Sentinels were there as well, standing just behind him as he talked to King Kandal and Goslin— who she could see had found himself a new sword.

"I trust you had a good night's sleep?" Blue asked when he saw Alyssa sitting on her mule. "The Clifflander's feather beds are famous."

"I did," she replied quietly. The Captains standing around the fire had stopped talking and were now watching her and Brett. It made her suddenly self-conscious.

"That's good," Blue replied. "Because it's most likely your last night in Tanzal, and I'm glad that you will remember it well. For good or for ill, today will be the end. We have come far together, Alyssa, and I have joyed in both you and your brother's company. Your love of life and the energy with which you live it makes my heart sing. You have also been brave beyond my greatest expectations, and your world must be a wonderful place if all those who people it are as courageous and happy as you.

"But now, my child, you must listen to me well: Even though I may not be with you physically on this last leg of your journey, I will be watching your every step with my magic. You may not see me, but I will be there. Take great caution while climbing, and do as Burrow tells you. Many forces will be at work today, some that we know about, and some, I fear, that we have yet to see—or feel their presence.

"I do not know how the Ancient One's spell will manifest itself, or even how it will unfold, so I cannot advise you on that, except to tell you to follow your heart. But one thing I *do* know is that it has already been triggered. Something in the night has set it off, and I can feel it hovering in the air all around me. It feels to me like a great wheel of power grinding inexorably forward. And one way or another, for good or ill, we are all going to be pulled along.

"Remember, Alyssa, today you must trust your instincts—and always, always, follow your heart!"

"I will," she answered quietly when Blue was done talking. "And thank you for helping us. I don't know what we would have done without you."

"The pleasure has been all mine," he replied. "And I honestly feel that it was actually *you* helping *me*, and not the other way around. If The Unicorns of Andwar are successful in this Great Task of ours, it will be due to you and your brother's aid. And all of Tanzal will owe you an unrepayable debt."

At this, for a long moment, everyone was quiet.

"Well, the time had come for us to ride," King Kandal finally spoke up, breaking the uncomfortable silence. "Burrow, have you arranged for climber's and scouts?"

"Yes," Burrow answered. "I have five of Cliffland's best climbers and her four top archers with me, and I have sent over fifty scouts on ahead to secure the Passage and tie off our ropes. Everything needed for a quick, safe and easy climb will be firmly in place long before we get there."

"Then I suppose that it is time to ride!" Kandal cried. "Call for formation, Goslin!

"Today, the Harriden will feel our wrath!"

For the next forty-five minutes the horns blew and the soldiers mounted their horses and fell into lines five wide. Most of the mounted warriors were swordsmen, but some carried long lances and even axes, while a few others in the front were the Standard Bearers. Almost all of the foot soldiers were archers, although most of them also carried a short sword on their hips as well. After saying his final goodbyes to Alyssa and Brett, Blue and the Unicorns of Andwar lined up in the front of the army and led the way out.

It was a full hour before the last of the foot soldiers tromped out of the meadow. Quietly, and with little fanfare, Burrow and his company of eleven riders fell in and brought up the rear. He had given both Brett and Alyssa their reins with strict instructions to stay close behind him.

"None of my mules dare kick each other," he told them quietly. "They know that I kick harder, so just keep your mule's head on my mule's butt, and we'll be fine. I don't want you far from me."

The group followed the army for a good mile or two before Burrow silently turned his mare to the left and made his way up a barely discernable trail. The path quickly wound its way into a stand of dark, tall pines that clung stubbornly to a steeply ascending, rocky hillside.

During the next two hours, Burrow set a fast pace and the mules climbed hard in the star-filled, pre-dawn dark. Their breathing was heavy and their necks and flanks dripped with sweat, but their strong uphill stride never faltered. Alyssa could tell that these mules were in good condition, as well as being well rested and well fed.

When the sky finally began to brighten, Alyssa could make out the trail that they were climbing. Although they were still headed almost due north, they had somehow circled around the mountain and were now climbing along it's west facing slope. The hillside below them was a steep, treeless jumble of sharp red rocks and boulders—a veritable rockslide waiting to happen—that fell away to a dark, mist-filled crevasse below. On the other side of this ravine, the sheer wall of the Impassable Mountains rose high above them. Only now, it wasn't nearly as tall. Alyssa figured that the mules had climbed at least half the height so far today.

The trail itself was a smooth, natural slickrock shelf that wind and water over time had cut in the mountainside. In places, it looked as if the Clifflanders had helped nature out by carving into the hillside increasing its width and height to accommodate a full-sized horse. As they climbed, the group passed through a series of alcoves and overhangs that prevented Alyssa from actually seeing the mountains above her.

For the next hour or so, the mules continued to climb steadily, and as they did, Alyssa noticed in the growing light that the farther they went, the more the cliffs of the Impassable Mountains were becoming less sheer and more broken with ledges and shelves. They were also rapidly falling in height, dropping down to meet the rising trail. The ravine between them was also rising rapidly.

"Hello, Burrow!" a voice suddenly called from the hillside above them. "You're early. We didn't expect you for at least another half-hour. I pity your mules!"

Alyssa turned in her saddle to see a good dozen men lounging among the rocks just off to the right of the trail. They were dressed in the same clothes that she and Brett were, and each had a bow close to hand.

"They love a brisk, early morning hike," Burrow retorted. "Anyway, they're getting fat and lazy, much like you. How's the trail and the Passage? Any problems this morning?"

"Nope. No problems at all. I personally climbed both faces and set the ropes and anchors myself. Everything's solid, and the Harriden are so busy digging themselves in around the base, I doubt they even know we're here. That wolf isn't going to climb with you, is he?"

"He's going to try," Burrow said, shaking his head and smiling in amusement down at Sturgill. "Okay, Alyssa and Brett, this is where we leave the mules and start hiking. Take everything you need, because we won't be coming back this way."

Alyssa slipped off her mule and pulled her small backpack from its saddlebags. She took a small sip from her water skin, re-loaded it in her pack, and then shouldered everything. She shifted the load on her back several times, to get comfortable—it was actually quite light with only her clothes, a magic book, a couple small Tanzalite rocks worth a king's ransom and a skin of water. Several of the soldiers collected the mules and led them away.

As he strapped on his own pack, Brett nudged her in the ribs and whispered, "Talk about Robin Hood and his Merry Men. These guys got it down pat! They come right out of the woodwork and scare the living crap out of you!"

"Shhh!" Alyssa hissed.

"Okay, listen up," Burrow said when they were all ready. "When we start climbing, Thomas will lead out and Tutwell and David will follow—our two top bowmen right behind our best climber. Acten will follow them, with Alyssa climbing right behind him. I'll follow Alyssa to anchor and watch her step and also lead Brett. Joshen, you'll bring up the rear of the "climbing team" and anchor Brett. Alyssa and Brett, be careful and follow in your lead's path and holds exactly, even when we're just hiking on the trail. If you have any questions at all, stop and ask. First and foremost a Clifflander is always safe! Sturgill, for the safety of the children, you'll need to come along behind Joshen. I'm sorry, but you can't anchor a human. Go only as far as you can get yourself back from, and be aware of the fact that I won't endanger this mission to save you. The remainder will bring up the rear, climbers first, archers second. Now step to it. Daylight's burning!"

And without another word, Burrow turned and strode quickly off down a narrow, rock-strewn path to the left of the main trail. The group fell into single file and followed.

At first the trail dropped quickly down, crossing the now shallow ravine. It wound its way through a field of boulders and stones before starting back up toward the base of the Impassable cliff face. On this part the group climbed hard for twenty minutes before reaching a small saddle where the ground leveled out. It was here that Alyssa and Brett got their first glimpse of the mountains that they would be climbing.

Towering high above them on the right were four tall, snow-tipped peaks. The first three were steep and sharp and very close together, rising from the same broad base as though they were fingers on a hand. Their sides were cut and craggy, with sharp ledges running between steep rockslides and sheer cliffs, and their snow-covered peaks were high and pointed, rising lonely into the cold, thin air. They reminded Alyssa of the Tetons in Wyoming.

The fourth peak, however, was completely different from the rest. It rose from a separate base, connected to the first three peaks by only a narrow saddle of land, and it was a round, almost cone-shaped, mountain with a wide, flat top. The sides of this circular peak climbed straight up in a series of shallow shelves that almost looked like steps. It gave it a kind of pyramid-like look.

"That's an extinct volcano!" Brett exclaimed.

"No," Burrow corrected him. *"That's* Spellcasting Peak. I've never heard of *Extinct Volcano* before, but it's not any mountain anywhere around here."

Brett began to object, but Alyssa cut him off in mid-sentence. "Don't worry about it, okay, Brett?" she growled. "Let's not argue about every little thing. And none of your free rock lectures, either. We haven't got the time for it today."

With poor grace, Brett shut-up and scowled at the ground. He was Mr. Geology himself, always full of *'fun and interesting'* facts about the rocks and mountains that their family climbed. If Alyssa hadn't have stopped him, Brett would have given Burrow a great big, long boring story about volcanoes and their plugs and how they were formed that would have put the entire group to sleep.

"The other three peaks are Daffonse, Narcinse, and Tulise, The Tall," Burrow added. "They are our Three Cold and Lonely Princesses. They are named for the flowers that grow on their bases during the summer months. Now, it's time to climb!"

For the next two hours, the party hiked steadily upward. The trail was jumbled and steep. Sometimes they trekked across narrow ledges abutting two hundred foot cliffs, while at others times they scrambled across rounded slickrock hillsides.

But always they went north and higher.

For this part of the journey, Burrow followed behind Alyssa and in front of Brett, keeping a close watch on both of them. Alyssa figured that he was looking for signs of stress, or a fear of heights. He was going to find neither. She and Brett were more at home doing this than they had been riding the mules in the dark.

By lunchtime, they had passed along the base of the first peak and come to a place where the hiking trail ended in a sheer cliff. Here, on a wide spot in the trail, Burrow called a break for lunch. A tall, stocky climber in the rear pulled a pack from his back and handed each of the group a small water skin filled with apple juice, two biscuits and a thick ham and cheese sandwich.

To the endless amusement of the Clifflanders, Alyssa broke her sandwich in two and fed the larger of the two halves to Sturgill.

"I'm afraid that you've reached the end of your trail," Burrow said to the wolf between bites of his own sandwich. "This is what we call The First Face, and I doubt that you can go any further. No four-legged creature could."

Sturgill smiled and nodded as he surveyed the cliff in front of them. It was at least a hundred feet high and fifty feet wide. Red and white ropes tied to steel anchors climbed in a diagonal across it before ending on the far side at the start of another steep, narrow ledge.

"I appreciate your letting me come this far," Sturgill replied graciously. "Obviously, I cannot climb that, nor can I fly, so it would seem that I am done. It's too bad—for me that is. I really wanted to see Alyssa to the end of her journey. But what will be, will be, and I know that she's in good company."

Suddenly, Sturgill turned and addressed the stocky Clifflander who had packed the lunch.

"Unless I'm mistaken," he said "You're Johanasson Dunt, aren't you?"

"Yes," the man replied slowly. He appeared irritated and even a little confused at this. "How would you know that? I'm sure that no one has spoken my name."

"Oh, I recognize you," Sturgill drawled. "I know—or maybe knew, I guess—your dog, Patches Dunt, very well. I considered her a good friend. But I haven't seen her out herding sheep in over two years. She didn't die, did she?"

Johanasson Dunt stared suspiciously down at Sturgill. Having a wolf claim to be his dog's *"good friend"* was quite obviously disconcerting to him—as was having him inquire as to her health.

"No," he replied slowly. "She's still alive, but she's getting old. She spends her days in my living room lying by the fire, but she's more than earned that. She's the best sheep dog I ever had. Also, she has some old wounds that she got as a pup that have been bothering her lately. She doesn't get around as well as she used to."

"Yes," Sturgill said thoughtfully. "I remember that day. It's been almost twelve years now, hasn't it? Did you know that it was a pack of wild wolves led by a Lycant that attacked her and those two older sheepdogs up near Goosehead rock that day? I could hear the fighting over a half-mile away, but by the time me and my pack got there, the two older dogs were dead and Patches was very close herself. We killed the Lycant and six others. The rest of the pack fled. It's too bad the shepherd working for you—what's his name, Taoson or something?—was passed out drunk. He could have saved those dogs. With guardians like that, who needs wild wolves!"

"He wasn't drunk," Johanasson objected strongly. "He fell and hit his head on a rock while fighting off the wolves. He even had a large red mark on his forehead and a black eye."

"No," Sturgill disagreed with a light chuckle. "He lied to you. He was drunk. Completely passed-out drunk. I smelled the empty jug myself. Cheep corn whiskey. He probably hit his head on a rock while stumbling around in a haze. We left him where he'd fallen, and I carried Patches on my back down to your front porch that evening.

Didn't you ever wonder how a ripped-up sheepdog pup with two broken legs walked home? And you do remember the loud barking at the door that woke you and brought you out, don't you? That wasn't your half-dead dog, that was I! And that's how I recognize you. I was watching as you picked up Patches and carried her inside—I stuck around to make sure you found her in time. I was always glad that she made it through, and we've been good friends ever since."

The group was silent for a few minutes, not knowing exactly how to take this. A couple of them were nodding and smiling, as though they knew about Taoson and this made perfect sense. But the rest looked mostly confused and skeptical. *Wolves* didn't defend sheep; that went against everything they'd ever been brought up to believe.

Finally, Burrow finished the last of his sandwich, washed it down with a swig of juice, then stood and stated firmly—as if to ward off any possible argument between the wolf and his men, "Well, I guess that mystery's solved. Everyone always wondered why the wolves didn't kill Taoson while he was 'knocked out' and then didn't kill and eat even so much as a single sheep once the dogs were dead. It never made any sense. I guess now we know the truth. But what confuses me, Master Wolf, is your age. If twelve years ago you were old enough to be a leader of a pack, you would be ancient by now, in wolf years anyway, wouldn't you?"

"The Talking Wolves are not the same as Wild Wolves," Sturgill replied. "They count their years the same as men. And, quite often, at times longer. A hundred-and-twenty-years-old is not unheard of for the leader of a strong pack. I won't tell you my age, and I mean no disrespect to you, but I will tell you this; I've been leading my pack for longer than you've been alive!"

"You learn something new everyday," one of the warriors muttered.

"So it would seem," Burrow answered. "But the time for learning from our wolf friend here is over, along with our lunch break, and the time for scaling cliffs has come. Thomas, go ahead and start climbing. David and Tutwell, you follow. Acten, fit Brett's harness to him while I fit Alyssa's."

153

It took Acten and Burrow only a few minutes to strap the climbing harnesses onto Alyssa and Brett. They then put on their own harnesses and using three twenty foot long ropes with clips on each end, hooked the five in the 'climbing group' together. Acten then clipped himself off to the first anchor, fingered his hold and began his ascent. Alyssa watched his path carefully. She might not be using his exact holds, being much smaller than him, but she would be taking the same climbing 'trail'.

When Acten was fifteen feet high, Alyssa stepped to the wall and felt the cliff's red stone. It was rough, like sandstone, but hard like granite. She reached up and tested her first handhold. It was a deep cut in the stone about five feet high that felt much more hollowed out than nature had intended. Her first foothold felt the same. She pulled her weight off the trail and reached above her head to the next handhold. It also was hollowed out to fit the contour of her palm and the footholds were perfectly placed.

This was, she knew, a climbing course but she hadn't realized that it would be this well improved.

"So the children really are going to climb," Johansson said in slight wonderment behind Alyssa. She didn't look back; she was too busy finding her next hold. "I had honestly planned on carrying one of them, Burrow, so perhaps—if you don't mind, that is—I'll carry the wolf instead. He certainly seems to want to go. And it appears that I owe him at least one ride."

"Suit yourself," Burrow replied. "But I've never heard of a Clifflander packing a wolf on a climb willingly. You may never live it down."

"Perhaps. But Patches gave me six of the best litters of pups that I've ever had, so if this wolf wishes me to carry him, I will, and hang anyone who thinks it odd! Johansson Dunt repays his debts! Even those he didn't know he had!"

"I would be grateful and honored," Alyssa heard Sturgill reply. She was in the middle of testing her next handhold so didn't dare look back, but he didn't sound at all surprised by this offer. She wondered if the wolf hadn't been planning this all along. He was at times as sly as Raspal.

"But," he continued, "I honestly feel you owe me nothing for my deeds. I am not like others who count all they do and hold it in their heads like a ledger of who owes whom, and for how much. When I act, I act from my heart, and if I feel that I am owed something, I will ask for it. I am a Talking Wolf, and for good or bad, we do what we do. Let those who sit in judgment think what they may, while the Wolves run free and live the life they love! However, I am not too proud to take a ride from you, if it is offered in this same spirit."

"It is," Johannason replied solemnly. "I will gladly carry you wherever you wish."

Alyssa was now fifteen feet high and she took a moment to glance back down. Burrow was preparing to start his climb—though still carefully watching her progress—while Brett was shifting impatiently back and forth on the heels of his feet.

"You're doing great," Burrow said. "The best I've ever seen from a girl your age. I'm impressed. But remember, you don't need to climb this fast. We have all day."

Turning back to cliff face, she replied, "I'm not climbing fast. I'm climbing slowly and carefully. You want to see fast? Let Brett go first! Then you'll see fast! He's probably gonna push you the whole way up, just like your mules on each other's butts! He drives my dad nuts."

For the next hour, Alyssa cautiously scaled the cliff. The holds on the diagonal course were firm and clean—hundreds of years of climbing had swept them clear of any loose debris long ago, much like many of the heavily used climbs in Arches National Park—but she still kept an eye on where Acten went in front of her. He was her guide. Several times she took a break and looked over her shoulder. Although Burrow was keeping a good distance between them, it was like she'd said it would be; Brett was right on his heels.

When she finally reached the top, Acten took her hand and pulled her onto the narrow ledge that passed for a trail up here.

"Move forward," he said. "We need to make room for the entire group. Everyone must be safely off the face before we go on."

A few minutes later Burrow pulled himself onto the ledge and then helped Brett up next. Joshen followed right behind.

"You two climbed very well," he said. "I'm pleased. It gives me hope for the next face."

"I've climbed Mall-Walls that were harder than that," Brett replied contemptuously.

"Indeed," Burrow said. "But, please tell me, what is a *Mall Wall*? I've never heard of them before."

"They're pre-fab, plastic climbing walls," Alyssa explained. "We have them in our world. They set them up in amusement parks, shopping malls, and places like that. They even have them on cruise ships anymore!"

"And their about as hard to climb as a set of stairs," Brett chimed in. "I quit doing Mall Walls years ago! I was hoping for a real climb."

Burrow laughed out loud. "I don't know what all this stuff you're talking about is, but a *real* climb, as you call it, you will soon have. The Second Face is just a short hike away, and should prove much more challenging."

Once all the climbers had made it up—and Sturgill was let out of Johannason's pack—the group continued on. Here the trail was barely three feet wide and they made their way much slower than before. At first, they skirted a steep, jumbled rockslide that fell for thousands of feet, reaching all the way to base of the Second Princess. Then, after that for about an hour, they scrambled along a series of ledges and shelves. On this part of the trail there was plenty of loose stone, as well as dirt and gravel, and Alyssa watched her step carefully because many of the falls they skirted were an easy three-thousand feet.

But, as her Dad always said, it didn't matter if you fell a hundred feet or three thousand, in the end you were just as dead.

When they came upon the Second Face, Alyssa could see what Burrow had been talking about. It was easily twice as tall as the first one—a good two hundred feet or more—and much smoother looking. Like the First Face, it was also a diagonal climb, though not as pronounced, and the red and white belaying ropes were already tied to it on a series of pre-attached anchors.

"We'll climb in the same order as before," Burrow said when they arrived. "Go ahead and start, Thomas. We'll be right behind you."

This second climb was indeed much more difficult than the first. Alyssa's holds were shallower, and more sporadic. She had to search and test them a great deal more, making sure that her grip was firm. Gone were the nicely carved and perfectly spaced holds of the First Face.

They climbed for more than hour, going slowly for Alyssa and Brett's sake. At one point, Alyssa glanced back and saw that all eleven of the climbers were on the face at the same time. Even though Sturgill probably outweighed Alyssa by at least twenty to thirty pounds, Johannason seemed to have no trouble carrying him, and the wolf, serenely smiling from his seat in the comfortable pack, seemed to be enjoying himself more than at any other time in this entire journey.

At the three-quarters way mark, Alyssa took a break to glance back down at Brett and Burrow, who happened to be watching her.

"You're doing great," Burrow said. "I guess we won't have to drop a rope for you after all. I really thought we would. I'm genuinely impressed!"

Smiling to herself, Alyssa turned back to the cliff and looked up for her next hold.

And that's when it happened.

For Alyssa, the first clue that something was wrong was the sound of a sudden howling all around her, like wild wolves, and the fierce whistling of rushing winds.

It startled her, and looking over her shoulder, she saw that all the climbers below her had their eyes tightly closed and their faces pressed against the cliff wall as wind-whipped sand blasted them and blew their hair and clothes wildly around.

But Alyssa felt nothing. Not even so much as the breath of a gentle breeze.

It was like she was in the eye of the storm. Protected. Untouchable.

At that instant, two things happened at once. First both her ropes, the one below her connecting her to Burrow and the one above her connecting her to Acten, were suddenly shredded and dropped to hang below her, and she saw floating in the air about twenty feet away, a strange vision.

It was like an open window, hanging in the air, or maybe, Alyssa thought, more like a floating mirror, reflecting a distant place. Either way, in the very center of this mirror, surrounded on all sides by a raging battle, stood Lord Falgerth. In his left hand he held his tall, gnarled staff with its blazing black jewel and in his right a fiery sword. His eyes were bloodshot and full of rage—and they were staring straight at Alyssa! They seemed to burn into her, burrowing into her very soul, searching her magic and touching an old memory. They were the eyes on the butterfly, she suddenly realized with an overwhelming sense of deja-vu. The large green butterfly that she'd seen in her front yard on the day this all started. Lord Falgerth had been looking for her even then!

But Lord Falgerth attention was only momentary, because behind him on the battlefield, Alyssa could see Blue racing toward him.

In the battles he'd fought before, Blue's hooves and horn had glowed with fire when he attacked, shooting sparks and flames. But now, the unicorn's entire body shone with power. He was the Flame of Andwar unveiled and in its full glory! Racing across the battlefield, he was like a blazing blue star fallen to earth, while directly behind him, ran his three Silver Sentinels. They also glowed with power, but theirs was white and pure and as brilliant as the sun—it was almost too bright for Alyssa to look directly at. They were like three Avenging Angels out for God's justice!

With a snarl full of frustration, Lord Falgerth turned to face the attacking unicorns. He lifted his staff and Leviathan's Jewel blazed darkly in its setting.

And then the vision was gone, along with the howling wind and blowing sand.

"The Queen's shielding has failed!" a voice said inside Alyssa's head. She gasped at it. It was the same voice that spoken on that first day, telling her about the Juxtaposition! *"But you are within my*

realm now, and I am shielding you. Trust me, my child, this shielding will not fail! But you must finish your climb on your own. Take no rope or help! Only you I can protect. If he attacks again, those around you are at risk!

"What the holy heck was that?" Brett exclaimed. He managed while clinging to the cliff with one hand to wipe the sand from his eyes with the other. "I thought it was going to knock me right off this climb, man! That was bad."

"The Queen's shielding has failed," Alyssa said. "And Lord Falgerth attacked us."

"But why did he stop?" Burrow asked. "We were at his mercy. We still are."

"From what I saw. Blue and his Silver Sentinels attacked him back. And from the looks of things, he has his hands full."

"Then we'd better get off this cliff face before their fight is finished," Burrow stated grimly. "Acten, scale as fast as you can to the top and drop Alyssa a rope. In fact, tie off ten ropes and drop one for each of us. We need to move, and fast."

"I can't take a rope," Alyssa stated quietly. "I'm still being shielded, but by somebody or something else now. Lord Falgerth can't touch me, but if I climb a rope, he could cut it and I could fall. The voice told me that I have to finish my climb by myself."

Burrow was quiet for a moment. "Then do what you have to do, Alyssa. But, please, be careful! The fall here is over a two thousand feet. If you lose your hold, all the shielding in the world won't save you!"

Thanks! Alyssa thought to herself. She turned back to face the cliff, glanced up for her next hold and allowed herself a moment of rest. She already knew that little piece of information and didn't need to hear it out loud. Not that it mattered. She wasn't going to fall. Everything was exactly the same as it was just a minute ago. The cliff hadn't changed. Nor had the holds or the path. Everything was fine. It was exactly the same.

Except now she didn't have a rope to catch her if she fell.

Alyssa was doing her first ever "freeclimb", something she'd swore she'd never do no matter how many years she climbed. Hanging by only one hand like Tom Cruise in *Mission Impossible 2* was for someone else—probably Brett when he got older—not her.

Alyssa's next hold was a foot up. She let go her lower hand and reached for it. It was a decent grip, not too deep, but still okay. She pulled herself up, shifted her feet, and then looked for her next. It was a little higher, but still well-placed.

She was going to be fine, she told herself. She'd done this at least a thousand times. She grabbed the next grip and moved slowly up. A light breeze brushed back her hair and cooled her forehead, while the afternoon sun beat down on her back.

As she climbed, Alyssa could hear the grunts of those below her, but didn't look down. She was done with checking to see how everyone else was doing. At least they were tied to the anchors. She was also finished with checking to see how much higher she had to go. She simply concentrated on her next handhold and nothing else. Everything else was just a distraction. She heard a crow call from somewhere far below her. It sent a chill up her spine.

Ten minutes later, Alyssa felt a hand grab her wrist and forcefully haul her onto the ledge at the top. She breathed a sigh of relief as she found herself sitting safely on solid stone. Glancing down she saw that Burrow was barely a foot below her, and Brett right behind him.

"I'd have caught you if you fell," he said as he pulled himself up as well. "And then we would have found out if my rope could hold us both. Luckily we didn't have to."

It took only a few more minutes before the rest of the group made it up to the ledge.

"Well," Burrow said as they took a short breather. "Falgerth knows that we're here and I'm sure he'll send up a contingent of Harriden warriors to attack us. But we should reach Kolvard's Steps long before they do. We'll have to set up some sort of defense. We'll do it where the trail is narrowest, right before the steps. Only one warrior can pass there at a time."

"Perhaps, the Harriden might be slow," Sturgill interrupted. "But I doubt that the Lycants he sends will be so also. Are there any cliffs left between here and there?"

"No," Burrow answered.

"So I could pass by myself? I no longer need to be carried?"

"You should have no problem. The worst in front of us is Leatham's Razor, but that is at least two feet wide even at its narrowest spot."

"Then I will see you at Kolvard's steps, where the trail will allow only one to attack at a time!" Sturgill called over his shoulder as he slipped between the men and dashed off. "I will hold the Lycants back for as long as I draw breath. They must not be allowed to block the way to The Steps. But make haste, my two-legged friends, because there is only one of me and there may be hundreds of them!"

"He's right," Burrow muttered as he watched Sturgill disappear around a bend in the trail. "There's no time for rest. Acten, tie off to Brett for the Razor. I'll tie off with Alyssa. Children, the razor is not technically difficult, but it can be scary. It may be the highest drop you'll ever see, but after watching you climb, I have no doubt that you'll do fine. Now, let's roll!"

For the next ten minutes the group skirted quickly around the last Princess. The trail here was a narrow ledge cut into solid rock that was in spots barely three feet wide. It was the only part of the path so far that looked as though it was completely man-made and it was fairly free of loose stones and dirt. As they rounded the last leg, Alyssa and Brett got their first glimpse of The Razor.

Leatham's Razor was a four hundred yard long fin of slickrock that connected the last Princess to Spellcasting peak. Here, they were now so high—almost near the top of both peaks—that the fall on both sides was over three thousand vertical feet.

"Don't look down," Burrow said with a laugh as he led them out onto the Razor. "You may never look up again! But, seriously, don't look down. It tends to make you dizzy, even if you've crossed it a hundred times."

Even without looking down, Alyssa found the world spinning slightly around her. The redrock fin was flat and smooth and in most parts between four and five feet wide, but it still seemed as though she were walking a balance beam across a huge abyss. Near the center, the Razor narrowed to only two feet, and it was here that Alyssa was assailed with a sudden dizziness. The world tilted and twirled. For an instant, it felt as though she were standing on the head of a pin hanging freely in space with blue sky and thin clouds whirling all around her. She felt Burrow's hand touch her shoulder and the world slowly stopped spinning.

"No one knows why that happens at this spot," he said quietly. "We call it The Veil, and it only affects a select few. Somehow, I knew it would touch you. It's worse for those with magic, and the more natural magic you possess, the worse it is. Take a moment to collect yourself. It will pass."

When the world finally stopped reeling, Alyssa looked up from the narrow ledge and smiled at Burrow.

"I'm okay now," she said. "We can go."

They crossed the last hundred yards of the Razor without incident. The trail on the other side was wide and flat and the stone that made up Spellcasting Mountain was brown and sharp and broken, like an old lava flow. It glinted in the sun with specks of micah and quartz. Here, the sounds of a distant dog-fight drifted to their ears.

"The lycants have arrived!" Burrow called to his men. "Archers, go help that wolf!"

The five archers dropped their packs, pulled their bows and sprang forward. They were notching arrows even as they ran. It was only a moment later as the rest of the group ran up from behind that Alyssa heard the distinct twang of arrows being released. This was followed by the several loud 'thuds' and the loud whining of an animal.

Alyssa was suddenly sure that Sturgill had been hit. As they came on the scene, she saw that he hadn't, but he wasn't in much better shape than if he had. The fur on his chest and front legs had been shredded and torn, and he was bleeding profusely from several large gashes. His ear was ripped halfway off and it looked as if one of his front legs was broken. One of the archers was tearing up his shirt while second used it to bind the black wolf's wounds.

Twelve lycants lay dead on the narrow trail behind him—and only three sported feathered shafts!

The rest of the pack of lycants had apparently run off at the sight of reinforcements.

"Sturgill!" Alyssa cried as she ran up to him. "Are you all right? You should have waited for help!"

"I'll be fine," he replied with a shrug. "Just a few scratches."

"No, you're not," the archer binding his wounds said gruffly. "You're on the verge of bleeding to death. Lay still!"

"But even if that happens, I'll still be fine. We all must die, sooner or later. My life has been good, and before it ends, I will get to see the girl-child reach the steps unharmed. Now, it is time for her part. She is where she needs to be!"

"But I don't know what I'm supposed to do!" Alyssa objected.

You must climb my steps, child. Turn and look. They are behind you. Alyssa whirled and stared intently. She saw nothing but a tall sheer cliff rising up to the flat of Spellcasting Peak directly above her. She saw nothing that even resembled steps, just sheer cliffs and ledges.

"I don't see the steps," she cried. "I don't see anything!"

Look harder, child! Look in the air. You must climb the steps in the air! You must stop **Time!**

Suddenly, almost like a vision of a floating angel, she saw the steps. It was a spiral staircase, hanging transparent in the air in front of her and framed in a sparkling collage of silver and grey magic-lights. It looked almost like a mirage, a sparkling vision of a crazed mind. She took a tentative step forward and climbed onto the first step.

"She's standing on air!" Alyssa heard Brett exclaim behind her. But his voice was now distant sounding and fading fast. The entire world was fading; her vision was rapidly filling with only the sight of the glittering, magical stairs.

"Yes," she heard Burrow answer, his voice also faint and far away sounding. "Kolvard's Steps cannot be seen without the aid of magic.

They are the stairs that aren't there! They are The Stairs in the Air! She has found them!"

Run, my girl, run! It's the only way to stop time!

And, suddenly, energy rushed through Alyssa, and she *wanted* to run.

It was *time.*

CHAPTER TWELVE

Healing the Shield

In a sudden rush, Alyssa sprang up the staircase. Her legs were filled with a strange energy, and her feet seemed to have a mind of their own. They felt as if they'd been given wings! They pumped faster and faster, tireless, and the sparkling circular railing and white marble steps—which were now as real-looking and solid as any she'd ever tread—climbed ever upward toward the summit. The cliffs and wind and clouds rushed past her as she ran ever higher, faster and faster, until they were nothing but a blinding blur.

But the strange thing was: the faster and higher she went, and the more the world whirled past her, the slower everything inside of her became. Her mind became calm and quiet and her sight and hearing became detached, almost as though she were standing just outside of herself and watching herself run. Now, everything—the entire world—seemed to fade, to become distant and slow. She felt as if something very large, something very *fundamental* was changing.

With a sudden jolt, Alyssa came back to herself with the realization that she had reached the top of the stairs—and that she was no longer running! She now found herself standing in a tall, domed crystal room, the walls of which glistened and sparkled with the colors of the rainbow, almost as if they were made of diamonds, crushed and rolled and then poured into clear crystal.

In the very center of this room stood a single, glass table with one glass chair. In it, with his back to her, sat an old man. His hair was long and white and hung down his back to almost his waist, and the robe he wore was also white and hung in folds over his arms and lap.

Slowly, the old man stood and turned to face Alyssa. His eyes, staring out from under thick, bushy eyebrows, were kindly and gentle, and his smile was soft and seemed to be filled with quiet laughter.

"Congratulations, my dear child," he said with a light chuckle. "You have stopped time for yourself. Only one other Mage in the history of magic has done so, and you are looking at him!"

"Are you…" Alyssa stuttered. "Are you the Ancient One?"

"I have been called that, at times. I have been called many other things as well, some of them not as complimentary as the others. Not all were pleased with my raising of the Northern Shield, but since I never asked their leave, it has yet to bother me. Evil people and things will always find someone or something else to hate, because if they didn't, they would be forced to look inside themselves and see the true root of their malice and loathing—themselves! My given name is Kolvard Astral Newhand. You may call me Kolvard. Your name I know; it is Alyssa Nicole Turner, because in a very real sense, I am the reason you are here. I am pleased to finally meet you in person."

"So you brought me here? I wasn't pulled through a Juxtaposition on accident?"

A shadow seemed to pass across the old man's face, and his gaze dropped.

"Yes," he said. "It was I who called you here. Or, more correctly, it was an error on my part—and in my spell—that dragged you across space and time. But, please, have a seat. Although the story may be long, we have time enough for it and any other you may wish, because in here, time moves not. But still, your legs will tire from standing."

The old man bowed slightly and nodded toward the table. With wonder, Alyssa saw that there were now two crystal chairs in front of the table instead of just one. Shyly, she walked over and sat down. Kolvard seated himself next to her and pointed to the crystal table in front of them. In it, embedded in white gold, she saw four large, dark green Tanzalite stones. They were size of baseballs and cut with a thousand sparkling facets that brilliantly refracted the light of the walls all around them.

"Before you, Alyssa, you see the Guardian Stones. They were the dug from the Starfire mountains ages ago. Ages, in fact, before even I was born. No Evil has ever touched them, and always they have been used in defense of all that is good in Tanzal. Their power is the foundation of The Great Northern Shield, though they are not actually part of the shield itself. They also aid the Wizarding Council at need.

"Many believe that the Northern Shield was my greatest shield, but they are mistaken. The Great Northern Shield has weaknesses and flaws, which evil has now managed to exploit, bringing it to verge of death. No, my greatest Living Shield is the one that you see all around you. It is a shield against time itself, aloof and flawless, built for the sole purpose of housing both myself and these greatest of all stones far from the long reach of evil until the time that we would be needed again!

"But alas, Alyssa, that brings us back to why you are here. Long ago, before I ever entered this timeless room, I foresaw that Evil, the true Evil of which Lord Falgerth is but a tool, would eventually wear away at my shield and bring it down. It was then that the First Wizarding Council and I cast a spell through time to search out a great Mage of Healing and bring him to us in our hour of need. Of course, most of the greatest Mages are born in Tanzal, because she is the strongest in magic of any world, so it never occurred to us to limit our search to our world. However, not given that parameter, our spell searched through *space* as well as time. And far out on the fringes of existence, on a world called Earth that is rife with Engineering and Technology—the killers and replacers of magic!—it found one of the greatest anomalies ever seen; a young girl with a huge unknown power. A veritable wizard on a world long bereft of almost all Mages and Magic.

"And then my spell forced a Juxtaposition on your world and dragged you through. Since then, since I realized my grievous error, I have striven from this place to keep you safe. Only those who live on Tanzal should be forced to fight for her or risk their lives in her wars. Fortunately, you have made it through safely, and now we are beyond evil's reach. Neither you nor your brother is in danger any longer.

"And now, together, you and I will *heal* my shield. Then I will send both you and your brother home."

"Okay," Alyssa said. "I kind of understand that part now. But tell me this, what is Brett doing here? He doesn't even have any magic!"

Kolvard chuckled and shook his head in amusement. "Now *that* was a true comedy of errors. At the exact instant of the end of the Juxtaposition, your brother was triangulated—that is to say that he was being held firmly at two points, by the Meadow Tiger as well as by you. He was the third side of a Translating Triangle. There was no way your world had the power to hold him, and he popped through along with you. I guess you could call him a cosmic stowaway on *your* magic carpet ride!"

"But if you didn't plan on him coming, then will you be able to send him home as well? I mean, he's not even here in the room with us!"

"I will," Kolvard answered confidently. "I have altered the Returning Spell to include him as well. When we are done, you will both be safely returned to your world, and no one will even know that you were gone."

At this, Alyssa shook her head. Now, he wasn't making any sense. Of course people would miss her and Brett. It was just plain crazy to think otherwise.

"How can that be?" she asked. "We've been gone for almost two weeks now. Did you cast a spell on my parents as well, so they'd think we're at summer camp or something?"

Kolvard laughed out loud. It was a pure sound, untainted by rancor or bitterness.

"No," he said. "I have done nothing as nefarious as that. It was actually much simpler. Although I cannot stop time for an entire world, I can, however, *slow* it down. Which is what I've done. Two weeks have passed on Tanzal while only a few minutes have passed on your world. No one will even know that you were gone, and I suggest that you and your brother keep this entire adventure to yourselves. I sincerely doubt that anyone in your world would believe you anyway. Even with all the wonders your vaunted technology can produce, such as electric lights that come on with the clap of your hands, even the slightest bit of real magic is viewed with great skepticism."

"Well, then, what do I need to do to 'Heal the Shield' so I can go home. Where do we start."

"First, you must decide that you *want* to heal my shield," Kolvard said. "I know that may sound funny, after everything that you've been through to get here, but that is the way it must be. This Healing Spell you will be casting, and your allowing me to help you with it, must be your choice from here on out. It must be purely voluntary. If you don't wish to do it, say so now, and I will send both you and your brother back to earth immediately, and hold no ill will toward you. My mistake may have brought you here, but under no under circumstances will you be forced to help Tanzal against your wishes as a condition of your being sent home.

"So search your heart, and decide now what you truly wish to do. Will you help the world of Tanzal and heal my shield?"

Alyssa didn't even have to think about this. She had always assumed that she would do what she could, but after all they'd gone through to get here, there was no way that she was going to leave this job undone.

"Of course I will. It's not like it's dangerous, or anything, is it?"

"No," Kolvard replied with a smile. "There is no danger left to you. Now, if you wish to help then take my Fourth Book of Magic out of your pack and lay it on the table in front of you."

Alyssa did as she was told. The book was warm to her touch and seemed larger and heavier than before. Ancient white ruins she hadn't noticed previously now crisscrossed the old leather, and the book seemed almost to throb in anticipation.

"Now, flip the latch holding it shut."

"Blue said that only a great magic could open this book," Alyssa objected. "Don't I need to recite an Opening Spell, or something?"

"The unicorn was indeed right; a Great Magic is needed to open that book. Over the years, the Norfs tried everything they could think of to force it open, hoping that by reading it they could find a way to thwart my return. But all their efforts yielded them naught. The Great Magic needed to open that book is in your fingertips, Alyssa, and always has been. You could have opened it at anytime—you had only to try! Now, go ahead. Open the book."

Alyssa reached down and gently touched the delicate silver latch. It sprang open with a flash of light and a loud 'pop' like a cap gun going off. She jumped back with surprise. Kolvard chuckled.

"I'm sorry," he said. "I forget that it was 'spring-loaded'. But now it is open, and it is finally my turn to strike! Evil has lost yet another battle!"

The old magician stepped to the table and eagerly flipped open the book's leather cover. Despite her natural fear, Alyssa leaned forward and looked inside. She had expected to see thick, aged paper with strange, dark ruins scrawled across it—and maybe a drawing of some kind, like a pentagram or something. Instead, to her extreme surprise, Alyssa found herself looking at a full color picture of herself and Brett standing in the meadow they had arrived in.

But the really crazy thing was, the picture was moving! It was like watching a high-definition 3-D movie of herself and her brother, only without any sound.

She watched as she and Brett first talked, than turned and walked together toward the distant forest. The tall grass around them swayed in the gentle wind, while the Meadow Tigers crouched and sprang among the dotted stands of flowers, hoping to catch their prey, the huge butterflies.

"Throughout time," Kolvard cried. "Everyone—even Tanzal's greatest magicians—has thought that *written* in the Fourth Book of Magic was the spells needed to restore my shield. Oh, how wrong they were! The Fourth Book of Magic *is* the spell needed to restore my shield. And it is even now working its magic! It is *opened*, and I am returned, for a brief moment of time. Take my hand, child! It is time to activate your magic, and together you and I will build the greatest Living Shield that Tanzal has ever seen!"

Timidly, Alyssa reached out and took the magician's outstretched hand. His skin was wrinkled and leathery, but warm. She felt an electric current run up her arm, much like when she had been attached to Blue and he had been drawing her magic.

"Altonian el Tonat!" Kolvard cried. "Let her power come forth! Let her Hands have their Healing!"

Alyssa suddenly felt dizzy and faint, and it was only the Ancient One's strong grip that kept her standing on her feet. All around her now, forest green magic-lights sparkled and spun. They filled her vision. They filled the air.

Then, as suddenly as they'd come, the dark green flying sparkles were gone. Alyssa's vision came quickly back into focus, but now she felt as though something very *fundamental* inside of her had changed. She felt as though she could *do* things—as though she had *power* as well! Her entire body tingled with anticipation, especially her hands and fingertips. A new lightness filled her—she felt like she could almost fly!

"It is time to go," Kolvard said gently. "I will lead the way. My shield awaits your Healing Hands."

The next part of Alyssa's time in Tanzal was—and always would be—little more than a blur. Still holding hands, together she and Kolvard seemed to turn and then lift from the floor and float toward the crystal wall.

"You are also a natural 'Ghoster'," Kolvard said as they lifted. "It usually comes with Great Talents—and you are no exception. That is what we are doing now."

Glancing back, just before they passed miraculously through the wall, Alyssa saw that both she and the Ancient One were still standing in the center of the room.

Then they were flying, faster and faster, down the mountainside. They passed over Brett, Sturgill, Burrow Handley and all his men. They were simply statues, frozen in time—bent motionless over the bleeding wolf as they bound his wounds. Next they flew above the fleeing pack of Lycants that he had defeated, also frozen in suspended time, and then the advancing troop of Harriden Warriors.

After that, they reached the bottom of the mountain and sped out across the lower plain. Everywhere below them were armed men and machines of war, row upon row, and all behind deep pits of burning oil. To Alyssa, the sight of motionless smoke and frozen flames was perhaps the most crazy of all.

Then, for just a brief moment—just before they passed out over the front lines of the Harriden army and started to skim across the Clifflanders—Alyssa thought she spotted Blue and his three white sentinels. They were laying on their sides, on the ground in a semi-circle behind enemy lines, and at their center stood Lord Falgerth, his hands held high above his head, clasping something silver in triumph.

Then the sight was gone as Kolvard's firm grip pulled her around and down, toward a dark line on the ground that was piled high with rectangular blocks of green light, each of which was about three feet long, two feet wide and a foot high. The translucent blocks were everywhere, thousands upon thousands, stretching in a heaped line from the distant seashore to the foot of Spellcasting peak and the Impassable Mountains. Kolvard brought them to a landing at the foot of this jumbled pile.

"Only in suspended time can you see the shield's stones," he said. "They are wounded badly, and near death, as are many other good and wholesome things in Tanzal at this time. The Keystone for *our* new shield—yours and mine—must come from Courage, Love, Empathy and Healing. Only you in all of Tanzal possess these qualities along with the Power needed to create Tanzal's first truly Flawless Shield. Hold out your hands, Alyssa, palms upward. It is time to form your Keystone, from your magic alone."

Alyssa did as she was asked and Kolvard placed his hands under hers, palms up, and then gently lifted. He slowly closed his eyes, a look of intense concentration on his face.

"*Septial al Mas,*" Kolvard said quietly, but with a deep, resonating power.

A quick, fierce energy suddenly coursed through Alyssa's entire body. She felt incredibly alive—and powerful. She suddenly, for no reason she could understand, envisioned her parents and felt a stab of overpowering love for them. Her father, strong and protecting, as solid as the rock mountains he had taught her to climb and always there for here whether it was with schoolwork or climbing, and then her mother, loving and gentle, but also as fierce as a mother hen protecting her chicks. She felt their love for her and Brett, their desire to shield them from all the evils in the world, pouring gently over her, like a high-mountain waterfall. She felt its power, its protection. It coursed up and down, across and through, coalescing in her hands.

In a daze, Alyssa glanced down at her hands and found herself holding a translucent block of light. Only this block was different from the rest. Where all the blocks lying around her were lime green—almost chartreuse—this one was a dark forest green, the color of waxed pine needles in a dense stand of pines. Inside, it sparkled and spun with a myriad of magic-lights. Her breath caught in her throat at the beauty of it. It was entrancing, magical—a green jewel in the shape of a block.

"Your Keystone is formed," Kolvard said quietly, opening his eyes. "And as far as I can tell, it is perfect. It was formed from pure love, and is meant only to protect—tall and strong and powerful. You must set it now. It must begin its job of protecting Tanzal."

Guiding her hands, Kolvard helped her gently set the block of light on the ground, in a east-west line running from the Impassable Mountains to the blue sea on the distant horizon.

"Now it is time to set my injured stones, to heal them, and use them to build the wall. Pick up any you wish and set them in the wall. Your touch is all they need—your healing will flow from your fingers on its own. You only need stack the blocks."

Alyssa did as Kolvard asked and began to stack the blocks. She worked in a haze, almost as though she were hypnotized, and every hundredth block or so, a sudden urge would strike her, and she would hold out her empty hands, thinking of all the beauty and wonder of Tanzal and another block of forest green would form on her open palms. She fitted it in next to the lighter blocks and continued on.

How long she worked, Alyssa could never fully recall. It may have only been an hour of frenzied stacking—or it may have been days, months, or even years. Time had no meaning here. Time didn't exist, and there was no way for her to measure what didn't exist. The haze she worked in seemed more like a dream than reality, and after all, how long were dreams? How long did you really walk in them. In the first moments of waking, when they faded slowly away as they always did, Alyssa could never tell. The building of the shield faded in her memory in much the same way.

In the end, all she could fully remember was one fleeting glimpse of the fully rebuilt Great Northern Shield stretching from the mountains to the sea and towering high into the sky, Kolvard's lime green walls speckled here and there with her dark green blocks. She was part of that shield, she realized. Her magic was helping to hold it up.

Then, suddenly, she and Kolvard were once again standing in the crystal room.

"You have done well," he said with a tired sigh. "And now we come to my final spell. It is time to send you home, and then I can finally rest."

Alyssa stared down at the floor and scuffed her feet. She suddenly didn't want to ask the question that had been bothering her ever since she had seen Blue and his Sentinels lying at Lord Falgerth's feet. But she knew she had too. She hadn't come this far under the unicorn's protection only to not know what happened to him in the end.

Mustering her courage, Alyssa glanced up and looked into Kolvard's care-lined, tired face.

"What happened to Blue?" she asked timidly. "I saw him lying in front of Lord Falgerth, and he was holding up what looked like Blue's silver horn. He said he would cut it off one day. He wasn't able to do that, was he?"

Kolvard sighed deeply. It was a tired sound, full of remorse and even, Alyssa thought, loneliness. His eyes dropped, his sad gaze fixing on the floor.

"I had hoped that you wouldn't see that," he said slowly. "I tried to turn you before you did, but somehow I always knew that it would come into your vision. Alyssa, you must keep in mind that both Blue and Sturgill were fighting for the world they love. Tanzal is many things, not all of which are good, but both of them gladly gave their lives in her defense. You must rest assured that they will, with their own eyes, see that their sacrifice was not in vain. Both of them are still alive, and they will sense our new shield's presence before they pass.

"Alyssa, they will be fulfilled. It was their world. It was their place to make the sacrifice, not yours. It was your job to rebuild the shield, and they did theirs so that you could do yours."

Feeling tears well up in her eyes and a lump form in her throat, Alyssa stared down at the floor herself. This wasn't supposed to end like this! Blue was The Blue Unicorn, the strongest ever foaled! And Sturgill, well Sturgill had just seemed indestructible, with never a shred of fear or hesitancy. She couldn't even imagine him dying. This couldn't be!

"How could The Blue Unicorn have lost to Lord Falgerth?" she asked quietly. "The unicorns were together again. They'd reformed Andwar. I know. I was there. And they had Lord Abigale and the Queen's staff helping them. How could he lose?"

Kolvard sighed again. "It was an almost perfectly matched duel," he replied softly. "And it will go down in the history of magic as one of the greatest. But Falgerth had Leviathan's Darkstone in his staff, as well as many dark powers from behind the broken shield. In the end, he barely prevailed, and now, even though he is almost completely drained, there is no power left on the field to fight him— and the unicorns lay at his feet. He has won that battle, but not the war."

"But couldn't I help Blue?" Alyssa asked. "I mean before you send me home. I am, after all, a healer, and for some reason I still feel like I have power left—a lot of it in fact—but I don't know. Maybe I'm wrong. The least I can do is save Sturgill."

Kolvard turned from Alyssa and looked away. He suddenly

seemed old and tired. His head was bowed; his stance slumped with fatigue. Shaking his head in resignation, he glanced sideways at her. His gaze was sad, and, Alyssa thought, very, very tired.

"Out of all the dangers that I foresaw would arise for both you and my Living Shield, this one, Alyssa, I knew to be the gravest of all. Let me impress on you once again that Tanzal's problems are not yours. You have done more for us than anyone on this world had a right to expect. Now it is time for you to leave, and let Tanzal take care of her own."

Kolvard didn't want to answer her question, Alyssa realized. But that wasn't going to be good enough. He was right in the fact that she'd done a lot, and even though she didn't want anything in return, she felt as if Kolvard owed her at least this. Sometimes her dad acted this way, and she knew how to handle it. You just asked your question, over and over again if you had to, until he answered it.

"But could I save Blue? And Sturgill, too? Do I have the power left? I mean, before you send me and Brett home?"

Suddenly, Kolvard turned and stared straight at her. His gaze was stronger and all the tiredness seemed to have dropped from him.

"What will be, will be," he said to no one in particular. "And there is no sense in fighting destiny. After all you have done I cannot lie to you, Alyssa, nor would I if I could. So I will tell you the truth. Yes, you could save Blue as well as Sturgill, but in order to do it, I must start time again. What must be done, must be done in Realtime, not the space we are currently in. And then, in the very short period of Realtime that my final spell will a lot me, I would have to help you with fighting Lord Falgerth and healing the unicorn. You may have the power left, but not the knowledge.

"But therein lies our problem. That very short period of Realtime built into my original spell was put there for me to use in sending you and your brother back home. If I use it to finish off Lord Falgerth and banish his Darkstone, I won't have any time left to cast the spell needed to send you home—which also must be cast in Realtime. You would be stuck here in Tanzal!"

"Forever?" Alyssa asked. "You mean that I'd never go home?"

Kolvard sighed again. "No, not forever. But you would be stuck here until the next natural Juxtaposition with Earth, and I honestly can't tell you when that would be. At that time, in the center of the next Juxtaposition, *you* would have to open my spells, first the one for your brother, and then yours, and *you* would then send *yourself* home. This would mean that you would have to learn magic while you are waiting for the Juxtaposition – enough, that is, to open the spells, which I would have to lock into two different Tanzalite stones. I believe you have two stones perfect for this purpose in your pocket right now, do you not?"

Alyssa gasped out loud. "I do," she cried reaching in pulling them out. "How did you know?"

"I foresaw this event. But now the time has come for you to make your final choice—and remember, Alyssa, you are choosing for your brother as well as yourself. His fate is in your hands! Let me once again strongly urge you to go home. Let Tanzal take care of her own! Blue and Sturgill gladly made their sacrifices, and would do so again without a second thought. *They* have won the war! They would want you to go home.

"Also, consider this as well, if you decide to stay, I will no longer be watching over you, or casting spells in your defense. You will have to fend for yourself, Alyssa. My final spell will be finished, and I, along with this place, will fade into history."

Alyssa thought about this. Having her brother's fate in her hands didn't really bother her as much as Kolvard obviously thought it would. Brett would be more than happy to stay longer here in Tanzal—especially if it was Alyssa's fault. Also, she was sure that Blue, Sturgill, the Queen and the remaining members of the Wizarding Council would help her while she waited for the next Juxtaposition—very powerful friends indeed! It wasn't like they were going to abandon her now that their use for her was done. They weren't like that; Alyssa knew this with perfect conviction. She knew it deep in her heart.

And really, what kind of danger could she possibly be in? The shield was now completely rebuilt, the war was basically over—at

177

least it would be after she took care of Lord Falgerth—and no one would be after her because she wouldn't be the key to anything, or have anyone's strange magic inside her!

It would basically be just like hanging out at the airport, waiting for a cosmic plane to take her home. The only real question was: How much time would pass on earth while she waited here? If the time on Earth was going to be too long, like days or weeks or even months, she would have to go home. She couldn't put her mother through something like that, not even for Blue. The answer to that was going to be the real clincher, she decided.

"Okay," she said quietly. "I have only one last question: If I stay until the next Juxtaposition, how much time will pass on Earth? How long will I be gone?"

"Once again, I will answer you truthfully, because I cannot lie, even though I know that the answer you seek will change your path.

"My original spell, cast long ago, will still be in effect, only it will be locked into those two stones you carry. I cannot give you a precise measurement comparison, because magic is not a science! But I can give you a very close guess. I would guess, and bet my life—or yours for that matter because mine is over!—that each year on Tanzal would be the equivalent of five minutes or so on Earth. Give or take a minute or two. I would also guess that the next natural Juxtaposition will take place a year from now, so the answer to your question is about six minutes."

"Then I will save Blue," Alyssa stated quietly. She really didn't need to think about it any more. She would be safe enough in Tanzal—the war was over!—and so would Brett, especially with his sword, and she would also get a year off from dance, chores, school and even homework. All for five minutes of being gone. It was a no-brainer.

Kolvard bowed his head. And when he looked back up, he was smiling wistfully. "I always knew that you would. It was destiny. Take the stones from your pocket, my child, and set them on the floor in front of you."

Alyssa did as she was told. The two large Tanzalite stones

sparkled brilliantly on the crystal floor, casting rays of faint green on the walls all around.

"Now listen closely, Alyssa," Kolvard stated solemnly. "You must remember everything I tell you a year from now, because once I am finished casting the spells into the stones, Time will start again and we won't be able to sit and talk. We will have to go straight to Falgerth and save the unicorn.

"While you are waiting on Tanzal for the next Juxtaposition, you must learn enough about magic to not only cast a very strong "Opening Spell" but also be able to control it once it has come out. This is very basic magic, and any accomplished magician will be able to instruct you. When the Juxtaposition arrives, Alyssa, there will come a time in the center of it when you will 'feel' that it is right. You will 'feel' the presence of your planet. At this moment, you will open Brett's spell and send him home. Then you will open your own, and send yourself home. Anyone else's presence at the spellcasting site may interfere with the spell. You MUST be alone. You will be able to take nothing but your original items back with you. Have nothing of Tanzal's on your person, because if you were somehow able to take something back, the Juxtaposition would not end until it was returned. It might even cause a Congruence with your world, Earth.

"Although Tanzal takes liberally from other worlds, she would never, ever, tolerate anything of hers being gone."

Kolvard paused for a moment, drawing a deep breath.

"Now Falgerth, on the other hand, I'm not so sure about. I know that he is almost drained of magic, but how drained exactly alludes me. He might still be strong enough to fight back in a small, mean way. I'm not sure. The only thing that I am sure about is that he stands absolutely no chance against you and I combined. However, having said that, I don't want to use all of our energy putting him into stone and healing the unicorn. I would honestly like to see you have enough left over to save Sturgill as well. So here's the plan.

"When I have finished putting my spell into your stones, our Realtime will start. I will hold out my hand, and together we will 'ghost' to where Blue and Falgerth are. Once there, the *very* first thing you must do is reach out and clasp your hands around that Darkstone in Falgerth's staff. Cover it completely, no matter how revolting its feel may be. I will then take care of the rest. I have banished Leviathan's Jewel once before, long ago, and I can do it again. After that, I will cast the spell that will put Falgerth into Judgement Stone. Remember, because of my spell, we are connected, even if we are not touching, and our magic will work as one.

"Now, are you ready?"

"But what about healing Blue?" Alyssa interjected quickly. "You haven't told me how I'm supposed to do that. Will you be casting that spell as well?"

Kolvard smiled in a quiet will *sense*, reflective sort of way. "No," he replied gently. "That will be for you to do. When you touch him, when the time comes, you will know what to do. You are a Healer, and you're magic is now active. You it, in much the same way that you sensed how to build your healing bricks for my shield.

"Now, once again I ask you, are you ready?"

"Yes," Alyssa replied quietly. "I'm ready."

Kolvard took a single step backward and lifted both his hands high above his head. He seemed to suddenly grow, infused with power, and Alyssa realized that in one of his hands he now held a long, crystal wand. It sparkled like a scintillating stick of diamonds, catching the room's light and bouncing the colors of the rainbow off its walls.

"*Lavicius Parrelysis!*" he cried loudly, and his wand glowed with a sudden burst of brilliant white light. Green magic lights instantly filled the room, swirling all around, sparkling chaotically.

"*En Estonian entrada!*" he finished as he lowered his hands and bowed his head.

In sudden concert, the magic lights began to spin counterclockwise around the top of the room. Faster and faster they went, denser and denser, until they were nothing more than a continuous blur of green light.

Then, to Alyssa's amazement, the lights separated into two swirling clouds, which condensed and lowered into the center of the room. Slowly two fingers of light descended out of the clouds, each pointing directly toward a different Tanzalite stone. They looked to Alyssa for all the world like twin tornadoes touching down. The funnels of light reached the top of the gems, which started to shine brilliantly, and began to enter.

Within only a few moments, the clouds had descended completely into the gemstones, like genies into bottles.

Without thinking—almost out of reflex, she would later think—Alyssa bent down and picked up her two stones. She rolled them around in the palm of one hand. They seemed heavier now, and at least two shades darker. They now looked a lot less like light green diamonds and much more like full-blown emeralds. Once again without thinking, she stuffed them into her pants pocket.

At that moment, Alyssa felt Kolvard's hand slip softly into hers and she looked up to find him standing beside her.

"Let us finish this thing," he said quietly. "Blue is waiting. And so is Falgerth. Time is now short."

Without another word, he turned and faced the front wall, and then they were off. The first time Alyssa had 'Ghosted', she'd flown fast over the ground but has still been able to see everything clearly.

This time, however, they went at superspeed, almost supersonic it seemed. They whizzed so fast that Alyssa could make out nothing at all below her. It was all simply a brown blur.

In only a moment, she found herself out in the center of the battlefield and floating gently behind Lord Falgerth, who was holding Blue's raggedly cut silver horn in one hand and his tall, twisted staff in the other. All around them stood Harriden warriors, holding their swords a their sides and watching the ritual intently. Blue and two of his Sentinels lay shackled at Falgerth's feet.

Cover the stone! Alyssa heard Kolvard's voice say inside her head. *Blue's time is short!*

Alyssa slipped her hand free from Kolvard's and reached forward and cupped the Darkstone in the top of Falgerth's staff. The feeling

181

of pure revulsion that poured over her almost made her faint. It took all her willpower to keep the vile stone covered. Later, she would think that it had felt much the same as though she had stuck her hands into a bag full of rotted meat—and been forced to hold them in while maggots crawled across her skin!

"*Ansal El Ostrally!*" she heard a voice cry—a voice that sounded strangely like her own! Alyssa suddenly realized that it was in fact her talking.

"Be gone, foul stone!" she heard her voice continue. "I have banished you before, and now I banish you yet again!"

With a sound like thunder, Falgerth's staff exploded into splinters and his Darkstone vanished. Falgerth himself fell backward and whirled around at the same time. His visage was twisted with a mix of sudden anger and fear. He barred his teeth like a cornered animal, and the hand holding Blue's horn dropped to his side.

Alyssa felt her hands rising and words forming in her throat. But before she could speak, Lord Falgerth grabbed the front of his dark cloak with his empty hand, lifted it over his face, and disappeared in a flash of light.

Just like in the movies! Alyssa thought in wonder.

It can't be helped, she heard Kolvard's voice speak inside her. *He had more power than I thought. He had enough to cast a Transporting Spell. He is beyond our reach now. There is nothing we can do about it, and our time grows very short. Tend to the Unicorn.*

"I've come to save you," Alyssa said quietly as she turned back and knelt down next to Blue. She cradled his hornless head into her lap, and then, casually, without even thinking about it, Alyssa waved her hand toward the ropes and shackles binding the legs of both Blue and his Silver Sentinels beside him. They broke and fell away like magic.

"I can't be saved," Blue said softly. "My end is at hand. My horn has been taken, and no unicorn can live without his horn—nor would he want to! We are creatures of magic, and as such, magic sustains our lives. When a unicorn's horn is removed, his magic drains slowly from his body in much the same way that your lifeblood drains from you if one of your veins is opened. I am dying Alyssa, but I go with the knowledge that my Unicorn's Quest, my purpose as a Blue Unicorn—my only purpose for being alive!—has been fulfilled. I sense that the Great Northern Shield has been rebuilt. *You* have given my life and now my death meaning, and I thank you for everything."

"You will not die!" Alyssa stated firmly. "I am a healer. And I am here to give you a new horn! And The Ancient One is here to help me."

And with that, on a sudden impulse, Alyssa laid her hands on Blue's head and thought about everything that he had ever done for her. Her love for him overpowered her senses. She remembered his kindness, his strength, and his firm but gentle guiding of her over the last few days. She felt her hands suddenly fill with power.

In almost the exact same way that her bricks for the shield had formed, a single horn began to grow on the jagged base of the Blue Unicorn's previous horn. It formed round and sharp and silver, with hints of green. It stopped the magical bleeding, and Alyssa suddenly felt her magic pouring into Blue, filling him, replacing that that he had lost.

When it was done, Alyssa fell backward with a gasp. The magical haze she'd been in slowly lifted and she now felt drained—and tired. But a sense of satisfaction filled her as she saw Blue struggle to his feet, his new horn glinting brilliantly in the sun. He had a look of pure wonder on his face.

"I *am* a healer, Blue," Alyssa heard herself say, even as the battlefield began to fade. Blue and his Sentinels staring in wonder at her now wavering 'ghost' were the last thing Alyssa saw as her power faded and her 'ghosting' ended.

I am done, my child, Kolvard's voice said inside her head. *My spell is over. You must save the wolf on your own. You will know what to do!*

And with that, Alyssa felt her magical bond with The Ancient one break and she found herself back at the base of Spellcasting Peak, where she had first started to climb Kolvard's steps. She whirled around to see that the group was exactly as she had left them. The large burly archer was just finishing the binding of Sturgill's wounds.

Striding forward purposefully, and without a single word, Alyssa stepped past both Brett and Burrow and gently pushed the warrior aside.

"Let me attend to him," she said quietly. "I am a healer."

"What's happening, Alyssa?" Brett asked in wonder. "Weren't you supposed to climb some steps, or something?"

"I'm done with that," she stated as she laid her hands on Sturgill's torn side. She could sense his life slipping away, even as the last of his lifeblood seeped into the ground beneath him. "And now I have to save Sturgill, so leave me alone."

"I can't be saved, Alyssa," Sturgill breathed softly. He lifted his head and gazed wistfully at her. "My wounds are too great, and my end is near. I can feel it in my broken bones. I am on my way to the Great Hunting Grounds in the sky. But it has been my great joy to know you, and to help in this greatest of all Quests. I can sense the Shield's presence. It's over, and we have won!"

"I just had this same argument with Blue," she said sternly. "And now he's probably dispatching Harriden warriors even as we speak—or accepting their surrender! Now lay still."

Sturgill's head fell back to the ground and Alyssa closed her eyes and concentrated as hard as she could. She didn't know exactly what she was supposed to do, or say, but she just *knew* that she could do it. She had to! Instinctively, she rubbed her hands back and forth across his torn fur.

Slowly, a light magical haze descended on her, and she could actually *sense* inside Sturgill. His bones were indeed broken, both his front legs, one of his hind, and even his back had a small fracture. She touched them with her mind, and felt them as she bound them back together. She then knitted his torn skin. It was ragged and ripped all over his body.

And then at the end, with the very last of her power, she poured lifeblood back into his veins. She didn't have the magical strength left to fill him completely, but it would be enough to save his life.

With a gasp, Alyssa fell backward and sat down hard. She was now completely drained of magic. She could feel it.

"Holy cow, Alyssa," Brett breathed in awe. "How did you do that?"

"Magic," she replied. "My magic has been activated. And it seems that I'm a healer."

"Wow, my sister's a witch doctor," Brett said, more to himself than anyone else. "So are you going to send us home now? Or is Blue? I mean, what's going on?"

Alyssa paused for a long minute, starring down at the ground. There was no getting around it, no sense in beating around the bush. She had to tell him sooner or later. Might as well get it over with.

"Brett," she said slowly. "The war's over. I've rebuilt Kolvard's shield. But, ah, I made a choice while I was doing this. And, believe me, I would asked you what you wanted, I really would have, but I couldn't. And so I chose for both of us. We're still going home…but, just not right away! Well, anyways, it's a long story, and I'll tell you when we get some time, but the short version of it is that we're going to be stuck here in Tanzal for a while. Maybe a long while.

"It might even be for as long as a year."

Printed in the United States
58308LVS00002BA/55